Playin' for Gain, Payin' with Pain

by
Donny A Wise

DORRANCE PUBLISHING CO., INC.
PITTSBURGH, PENNSYLVANIA 15222

This is a work of fiction. Names, characters, places, and incidents are ceither the product of the author's imagination or are used fictitiously, and any resemblance to actual persons, living or dead; events; or locales is entirely coincidental.

ISBN-13: 978-0-8059-7195-8
Library of Congress Control Number 2006921027
Printed in the United States of America

First Printing

For information or to order additional books, please write:
Dorrance Publishing Co., Inc.
701 Smithfield Street,
Third Floor
Pittsburgh, Pennsylvania 15222
U.S.A.
1-800-788-7654
Or visit our website and online catalogue at www.dorrancebookstore.com

Dedication

First and foremost I thank Jesus Christ. He died for me and I will forever worship his spirit. To my children, Dan and Madison, I hope you are proud. To Ma, Mova, Dad, Kelly, Rock, David, T.J., Branden, and Co-co, I love ya'll dearly. To Kevin and Ike, I thank God you guys saved me. Shout out to Greater Harvest Baptist Church, Matt, Danté, Mike, Craig, Damon, Lil Rock, Sydney, and Zola— this for all ya'll.

Chapter 1

"Thank you, Jesus!" I exclaimed as I pulled into the driveway when I saw the half piece of Dutch Master hanging from his lips. The nigga didn't smoke all the herb.

"Nigga, I thought you forgot," he softened. "It's almost 9:30." I could tell it was the soft, lean approach. He wanted to say more but realized that a free ride to Delaware was hard to come by.

"Chill, dawg. Can't a brother get a little morning exercise?" I joked before he got in and we took off.

We pulled into the gas station.

"Yo, since I don't got no dough, grab two Dutches. I gotta twenty bag." Now that's the shit that irks me. A nigga will take his last to buy some weed and think smoking wit' you is compensation, but the thought of a morning high brought a smile to my face.

"Can I have 20 on 6, two Dutches, and a pack of matches?" I recited as I approached the counter.

"Um, excuse me, sir, but can I see ID, please?"

"Man, damn. I left it in the car."

"Okay, next time you bring. Twenty-two fifty."

For such a fucked up accent, he sure pronounces money very well, I thought, tossing him twenty-three dollars. "Keep the change for the inconvenience," I retorted.

I grabbed the cigars and matches.

"Dank you have a nice day," he lied.

Like any friend that felt sorry he didn't pay for gas, Steve was already waiting by the pump, the old ass-kiss move.

"Which one?" Premium?" he suggested.

"Naw, regular. All the shit all the same, except the price," I responded.

"Here, spark this half a piece up." Now he was really being nice; Steve was the type you had to break his arm to get him to pass the bud. Now he's voluntarily offering.

I quickly reacted before he could change his mind. "Where da weed?"

As we pulled onto I-95 North, I began explaining my evening in between halls of smoke.

"Yo, I fucked the shit outta Toni last night," I lied. "Toni Washington, wit' the big ass and little titties."

"What nigga? Put me on, she a freak," he reasoned. The high was strong, added that to the fact that I hadn't eaten since yesterday afternoon. I began to wonder about my business. It has been three days since I finished my package and the re-up man Lenny had yet to contact me.

" I wonder when I'll get some more weed," I asked aloud.

Knowing the answer, Steve asked, "You still ain't got no weed?"

"Nope. You bought the last ounce and L is on hold; I wish he'd hurry up, I'm losing money." I could tell I had upset his plans. The plan had been to take a half pound of weed to Delaware, for Steve convinced me to front him. He was in desperate need of money and I knew that.

"So what am I gonna tell my peoples?" he asked genially.

"Tell them shit is on hold. Make them think it will be well worth the wait," I answered.

As we approached the toll booth exiting Maryland, I began to regret making Toni leave. One minute I'm telling her I love her, next minute I'm telling her I don't leave women alone in my apartment.

"But the motherfucker empty," I could recall her saying. "What the hell? I'm a steal ya refrigerator and stove? You probably gonna have another bitch come over when I leave," she bitched as she dressed in the scanty outfit that attracted me to her last night. *Well fuck it*, I thought. Rules are rules, and just because she fucked me extremely well on the first date doesn't make her an exception.

It was 10:06 when we exited the toll. I could tell Steve was becoming antsy, but he knew the last-model Acura contained the performance to get him there on time.

"We'll be there in thirty minutes," I said as I saw him peek at his shock watch.

"Yeah, that's what I was thinking," he lied.

I shifted the 2.5 TL into drive four and exploded into the fast lane so as to assure him I meant business. I was proud of Steve, going from robbing and stealing to enrolling full time in college. The least I could do was get the guy there on time. I put the car on cruise control at 70, turned to 92Q, and drove into a daze, only thinking about the road that lay ahead.

At 10:48 I pulled into the grungy parking lot of dorms. Steve was sound asleep, evidence that the high had gotten the better of him.

"Yo, get your ass out my car and go to class, nigga!"

He suddenly awoke to his familiar surroundings. "Yo, my nigga, we made it. You coming through for a minute or what?"

2

"Naw, I left my pager and cell phone at home and Lenny might be calling, "I explained.

"All right, holla back when you see, dude. You know I'm hurting for some paper," he reminded. "No doubt, and give him the one love pound and shoulder bump."

As he walked, staggering toward his apartment, I thought silently, *Whatever class he goin' to, he going' to fail.*

"Now back to business!" I yelled to my car. "Get Daddy home so we can make some loot-ay." I inserted Makavelli and programmed the CD player on repeat, song number 2. Steve was so high off the hydro, I decided the second blunt was overkill, so I stashed it in my ashtray for the ride home. I dug through the ashtray until I felt its remains. This was just what I needed for this song. I blasted *"Hail Mary"* and thought to myself, *Now this is living.*

The drive was long, very time-consuming, but very relaxing. I stopped at a Tasty Foods restaurant—my favorite—and ordered my favorite entrée: curry chicken and brown rice, smothered in curry gravy, with collard greens and cabbage sprinkled with salt and vinegar as my side orders. I washed the delicious tray down with a half-n-half of lemonade and iced tea and a feeling of divinity overcame me. A devoured platter of empty bones and rice particles stared up at me. *Damn,* I thought, *I gotta stop eating so damn fast.* I ordered a refill for the drive home and disappeared down Park Heights Avenue, heading to Cedonia. "I'm ready to sell some weed," I confessed as I looked at my watch.

As I entered my apartment, a feeling of loneliness suddenly overtook me. The empty walls cried for decoration. *Well,* I reasoned, *I've only been here three weeks, give it time.* I flopped on my unmade bed; it reminded me of last night. An empty bottle of Remy Martin lay next to a kicked-over ashtray; two burned roaches peeked out from underneath. I grabbed the pager; no pages. The cell phone screen displayed one missed call. It was Steve's number, timed 9:14 A.M. He was probably calling to bug me about my whereabouts. I withdrew a Dutch from the remaining box of fifty. *All I do is smoke and sell weed,* I sadly reasoned. *My life is so incomplete and lonely,* I thought as I stared at my studio apartment.

I reached for the phone to call Toni. Maybe she'd be willing to come back over, I thought. I began to slice the Dutch with a razor as I put the phone on my shoulder. No answer. *Bitch probably out getting fucked,* I thought jealously and hung up the phone. I began to spread the light green substance throughout the blunt.

"This is really getting old," I said to myself. "When is it gonna end?" I surmised as I perched the blunt on my lips. I closed my eyes and slowly sparked the el.

Why was I so depressed, I began to wonder, dragging on the blunt. Something has got to change, I kept thinking as a slow feeling of euphoria overcame my mind state. The vibration of my pager broke the half nod I had gone into; an unfamiliar number flashed across my screen with a code of $425 followed behind it. Somebody wanted some bud, I guessed and grabbed the phone to disappoint him or her.

"Cream," a voice blurted after a short ring, "wuz up, Baby?"

"Who dis?"

"Fats."

"Wuz up, fat ass?"

"Nigga, when you gon holla?" he asked.

"Nothing right now, Mo, but I'm a get with' you in an hour," I bluffed.

"Man, you said that yesterday. Man, fuck it, I'll call Sonny," and the phone went dead. "Fat fucka," I cursed to myself when I realized he'd hung up.

Who the fuck is Sonny? I wondered. *That's the fifth person I heard say his name. Who the fuck is getting all my clientele?* I hurriedly called the number Fats had paged from, hoping to get more insight. The phone rang endlessly until some old lady answered.

"Jimmy?"

"Naw, I'm looking for Fats," I said.

"Baby, this a pay phone and unless you f—" I hung up before she could finish.

Bitch, I ain't pressed for rap, I thought as I continued to wonder about the name "Sonny"—the one everyone was running to. *Fuck 'em all,* I thought as I unlocked the Brinks Portable Safe. I recounted the ten thousand dollars I had for the seventeenth time. I counted out 4400 from the collection and took the money into the bathroom. I removed the small amount of hydro I had left over in the safe. Damn, my stash was getting low. I reached under the sink and removed the bubble bath. I quickly rolled a small stick of reefer and rationed the amount I had left. I began throwing the hundreds into the bubbles as they filled the tub. *If a $4400 bubble bath doesn't make me feel good, nothing will,* I figured as I quickly undressed and lit the reefer. As I tiptoed into the water, I noticed the cold water was beginning to dominate. *Cheap hot water heater,* I thought as I settled in.

Why do I feel so lonely? I quizzed. I had money, women, a nice car, a fair share of friends and acquaintances, and my own apartment. I had all the latest fashions, from Akadems to Iceburg to wear designed by hip hop artists. Why did I have such a lonely void in my heart, I asked myself, knowing I didn't have an answer. With the big faces of dead presidents matted on my chest, I discontinued the flow of water and tilted my head back. Moments later, I nodded into euphoria.

After a brief and cautious nap, I was awakened by the phone ringing. *Yes! Somebody cares,* I thought. Sounding unfazed, I answered.

"Donny."

"Hey, Ma, what's going on?"

"Nothin'. You know why I am calling?"

"Why? What time is it?" I asked her.

"3:30," she responded.

"Oh yeah, you wanted me to go to church, but Ma, I am tired. I just walked in the door from taking Steve to Delaware," I half-truthed her.

"Aight. But you promised last week. The reverend is preaching about young people needing to get more involved with God. Girls gon be der. He told everybody to bring they kids." *Nice bait, Ma,* I thought, but my mind was made up.

"Where's Rock?" I inquired, knowing the answer to my own question.

"You know your brother ain't gonna go nowhere near no church. Besides, you know he say he's a Muslim, so worry about yaself. You going' or not?"

"Naw."

"Okay bye!"

"Ma, call and tell me how the service went," I said, trying to take the sting outta my rejection.

"No! You really need to come see for yourself," she fired. My attempt had done more harm than good.

"Maybe next time, Ma."

"Bye, Donny," she said and we hung up simultaneously. One thing about my mother was she loved the Lord. Everything she did, good or bad, had some type of spiritual reasoning, but she never degraded smoking her herb, which made me believe it was not a sin. We smoked together on occasion, which made all my friends envious. They had to sneak weed in and out of the house, but not me. My brother and I could smoke in the living room while my mother listened to gospel in her room. Only once we got in serious trouble, when she brought someone home from church, but what really made her mad was that we didn't save her any.

The bubbles had deflated, the water had become cool lukewarm, and the money lay sporadically around the tub. I dried off and walked nude to the unlocked safe with the dripping wet bills in my hand. I folded and secured them with a rubber band and returned them to the safe. The effects of the hydro left a drooly residue pasted outside my mouth. "The rest I'll save for a special occasion," I murmured as I closed the safe.

Like any loner who lives with a habit, I went to check to make sure everything was where I left it (even though I didn't move anything). I checked the cupboard for the stainless steel .380 I had recently bought. In actuality I was scared of guns, but it was a sign of the times to have one. I pointed it at an invisible target and pulled the trigger. The thought of an explosion made me close my eyes as I returned the gun to its place. I went to my regular stash of weed, which I kept separate from the hydro weed. It was enough to hold down my smoke habit until I re-upped. I recounted the remaining eight Dutch Musters. I knew they'll be gone by the morning. Tomorrow was Monday, the day I always bought a fresh box of 50 Corona Deluxe Masters to last me all week. The thought of smoking so much weed made me laugh as I banged my lungs of steel in my chest.

In my own little world I heard repeat buzzing; it dawned on me my pager had been on vibrate all this time! I dove on my bed and rumbled around until I found it. Eight pages! Yes! Somebody cares! As I went through them, six were from the same number. My nuisance-ass baby mama, who probably didn't want a damn thing. But the seventh and eight were Lenny. "Let's get ready to rumble!" I declared as I danced in front of the mirror. Selling weed was my life; it gave me prestige amongst my peers, and it made me feel important. People considered me to be a baller, a name associated with high-class drug dealers. I called the number.

"Len. Wuz up? Meet you at 9:00? Same place. Aight. Yeah, yeah, same thing. Peace," and I hung up the phone. After three days of feeling sorry for myself I knew it was time to go back to work.

Chapter 2

We arranged for the usual spot to be Tasty Foods; we both enjoyed curry chicken. Len was always late, so I didn't leave my apartment until 8:50 P.M. I arrived at a quarter after nine and, as expected, Len was nowhere in sight. I decided to order a double order of curry chicken. I simply gave the Jamaican woman a nod and held up a peace sign to indicate the number of orders. I felt good that she recognized me. The other people waiting for their orders silently stared and assumed I was known.

Len came at 9:28, and he looked very relieved to see me still there.

"Everything's in the trunk, inside the Foot Locker bag," he whispered. I nodded while wiping curry gravy from my mouth.

"The money is already inside your bag of food." It was a repetitious act. I would leave my car door open; Len would spot the car, deposit the package, and meet me in the restaurant. I would put the money in the bag of food and wait for him to arrive. It was a trustworthy way of doing business, but Len was old-fashioned. He never shorted me a gram and I never shorted him a dollar.

"How was your weekend?" he would ask to knock the edge off the business at hand.

"Got some pussy, went to Delaware, and sat around waiting for you," I answered honestly.

"Yeah, that shit was well worth the wait," he said, reminding me of what I had told Steve.

"I'm sure it is. Listen, I gotta go take care of business. I'll holla at you soon," I said to him as I started toward the door.

"Be careful, Shorty," he whispered as I exited into the pitch-black night of spring. I did my usual routine before taking off, calling up potential sales for five minutes. Really, it was a stall move, in case the police were surveying the transaction. I paged my ten best customers, hoping I would still catch a quick thousand before midnight. Suddenly my cell phone came to life.

"Hey, wuz up? Yeah, it's all good. How much? Aight, be there in twenty minutes." At that time, my page sounded. It was the old man, seventy-year-old Pop Martin. He never talked on the phone. He would page, put in 70-850, his code and amount he wanted to spend. My job was to get there in ample time.

Then I pulled off, for I had immediate business to attend to. I received another page on the way to Pop's house, an unfamiliar number followed by consecutive 911s, which usually means emergency but also was a ploy to get an immediate return call. I dialed the number while weaving through traffic.

"Who dis?" the receivant answered.

"Somebody page Cream?" I said.

"Shorty! Yo, this Steve. Wuz up, nigga! What the hell you?"

"How the hell you? Man, where you at?" I was finally able to ask him.

"Listen, I gotta ride back 'cause I an't staying up there broke. Did you get on yet?"

"Naw," I lied.

"Well I gotta drop on the heist, but I need ya car and a joint— "
I cut him off. "Yo, I'm not lending you my gun—it's brand new—and my car? You're crazy," I scolded.

"But it's gonna be easy, you won't have to do nothing but—"

I cut him off again. "Who, Steve? What white boy you plannin' to jack, huh?"

"Some white kid named Sonny. I hear he got five pounds and four thousand dollars stashed over some bitch house," he replied.

That was the one name I felt I could benefit from if he was robbed, but I knew it was wrong. "Oh yeah, Sonny. That four thousand dollars belongs to me. My people been running to that bitch for three days. Be at my house in an hour," I said with a tyrannical laugh and hung up.

Oh Sonny boy, huh, I thought. *I bet he won't see anymore weed in my town*, I laughed as I pulled up to Pop's shaggy habitat. He was sitting on the steps playing Solitaire. His suspenders showed his age and the navy blue Khakis were filthy. His brown eyes now carried a bluish tint and his light gray hair begged for a trim.

"What's cookin', good lookin'?" Pop asked as he saw me.

"Hey, Pop, I was running around."

" I been callin' that damn remote control of yours since yestadee. Ever'one down the home is low," he whispered.

I hastily walked back to the trunk of the car, trying to give the impression that I was in a rush. I briefly scanned the artifacts and stuffed one of many down my pants. "Come on Pop, I'm in a hurry," I stated, as he had yet to move. I hated going inside; ever since Ms. Martha died, Pop lived like a slob. Roaches and mice controlled the kitchen, the house was a mess, and a strong stench of mildew and wine filled the quarters, a sour combination.

"Let's go inside," Pop said. A heavy sigh escaped my lips.

"Pop, I'm in a hurry." He only paid in ten dollars bills, a trait from selling only dime bags. He counted the money twenty times it seemed. *Shit, for eight hundred fifty dollars, I can stand the smell,* I reasoned. I took a deep breath and stepped inside. Fifteen minutes expired before I stumbled back out onto the porch, gasping for breath. I felt as if there were hundreds of roaches crawling all over me.

"Damn," I said aloud as I counted the money, "even the money stink."

I entered the car and heard my pager buzzing. From the large consumption of weed and moving hastily, I always forgot to carry my pager or I would put it on my lap and drop it on the ground as I exited the car. "Oh shit. Mrs. Francis." I had told her twenty minutes. Now Mrs. Francis was a schoolteacher who bought a quarter-pound of weed on a weekly basis, solely for personal use. More unusual was the fact that she was white and married to a councilman. I hated riding to her Roland Park residence; my dark tinted windows were always studied by her neighbors, who looked out their windows every time they saw my headlights it seemed. My car stood out in the conservative neighborhood. I grabbed my phone and called her.

She answered, acting as if she was agitated.

"I'm ten minutes away. I had an emergency," I told her, a line that I had used many times, "and Mrs. Francis, it's $4.25 this time," I said to her to take some animosity outta her. I sped down Cold Spring Lane, the thought of robbing this kid Sonny filling my stomach with curious but skeptical butterflies.

I arrived at the residence five minutes later than promised. All the downstairs lights were off, but the bedroom light still shone bright. I scurried to the front door and saw the door was cracked. Mr. Francis knew his wife smoked, but he never imagined her connect being a nigga. Mrs. Francis was waiting in the dark, on the couch, her bong sitting anxiously beside her.

"Shhhh," she said before I spoke, "Michael's sleeping." We exchanged hands quickly and she gave me an old lamp to take out with me.

"This is to throw the neighbors off," she giggled as she closed the door behind me. Her dark shadow reminded me of a Frosted Flakes commercial, trying to hide her face while revealing her guilt.

I jumped into the ride and smiled. $1375 in an hour. Making the money reminded me how well I had established my business. I never made less than one thousand dollars a day. I wanted to disappear, because I knew Steve and some hard-up fuck boy waited at my house. Steve never did capers by himself; he always talked some dummy into helping him, then he would only pay the guy 25 percent, claiming to do all the work. "Fuck it," I said as I turned onto Cold Spring Lane. "I won't be wit' 'em.

To confirm my fears, Steve and some clown waited impatiently out front of my building as I pulled up.

"You ready, nigga?" I could hear Steve saying, Hold up—*I need to go inside,* thinking about the eight and a half pounds on me.

"Hold on," I said, "I have to take these tennis shoes inside." I said this to throw the new guy off as I gathered up my Foot Locker bag and entered the apartment lobby. I waved Steve to come up as I passed the stranger, who called himself Pistol.

When we entered an embarrassed grin covered my face. Empty bottles, unmade bed—the place was a wreck.

"Who dat?" concerned, I asked Steve.

"Uh, dude Pistol. He from my school. He cool," Steve answered as I frowned. I hated lending out my new stuff, especially to strange out-of-towners. I went to the cupboard and removed the Davis .380 and inserted six hollow-point Talons into the clip and fastened it. I hesitantly handed over my pistol to Steve.

"Yo, don't lose my shit and don't kill that motherfucker unless life depends on it," I warned him.

"Yo. . . ." he started, but I cut him off.

"You hold the joint, I don't know that nigga," I said, and before I knew it, I felt myself going against everything I had said before. "I'm not letting ya'll use my car without me. Fuck it, I'm going," I stupidly said.

"Come on den, nigga," Steve said excitedly.

"Hold up! What's the plan?" I asked him.

"Pistol is going to knock on the door and ask to buy a pound. He'll show the 'G' to make them think he is legit. While inside, he will examine how they operate. They are expecting a guy named Chris from Towson, so they'll think it's him. He will page me from inside there and punch in the number of people in the apartment. After we get the page, we'll go up and knock on the door. When they ask who it is, we'll say 'Chris's friend,' and when they open the door, just bumrush it." By the time Steve had finished mapping out the plan, I had finished rolling a Dutch.

"Let's smoke this shit on the way," I suggested. *That shit should work*, I thought.

"Pistol, this is Cream, my right-hand man," Steve explained with emphasis.

"Yeah, I seen him drop you off this morning," Pistol said as he flashed a mouth full of cheap fronts. As we drove cautiously through the city, the blunt burned perfectly. I started to blast DMX on the CD player but abruptly turned it down.

"You ain't scared, is you nigga?" I asked Pistol as I looked in the rear-view, in an attempt to relieve my own fears about this mission.

"Nah, nigga, is you?" The snap back made me laugh unexpectedly. He couldn't have been more right.

"Steve, you answer that," I said, hoping to move the weight to him.

"Nigga, we been doing this shit for years," he said confidently.

As we pulled into the well-kept parking lot of Southwood Apartment Complex, my leg began to shake uncontrollably. I knew the heist was about to begin.

"You remember everything, right?" Steve rehearsed and briefed Pistol—I mean, "Chris"—on his duties. "We're going to be in there, so don't panic," he assured him. Pistol was no stranger to armed robberies; his fiery eyes grimaced with delight at the thought of the seizure.

"We'll be parked over there on Chestnut," I told him as he got out and slammed the door.

"Asshole," I hissed under my breath. I began to ponder the idea of being caught. I didn't need the weed or the money, and that's usually when shit went wrong. But I couldn't allow them to use my car and my gun without me overseeing how they handled my expensive possessions. A car or a gun could always bring fast cash, and I wouldn't lose both without my supervision, I tried to reason with myself. But inside I knew I had made a mistake. These types of actions did not fit my pedigree. I took pride in being honest and objected to taking from the weak. I felt I was smart enough to make money without harming and hurting anyone. This decision contradicted my character.

We parked at an angle so we could see directly inside the apartment, which was on the third floor. We saw some blond-haired dude immediately rush to the door and greet "Chris."

"Is that him?" I dumbly asked.

"I don't know," Steve responded equally. Confirming the heist was thought to be a jinx on any caper, so we stayed quiet. Suddenly Steve's pager gave off an annoying ring.

"Shit. Four," he relayed to me as my legs began to shake like Jell-o again. Steve withdrew the pistol and fitted the black gloves on his fingers.

"Gimme my mask," I said, hoping to alleviate my cowardice. Steve removed a colorful top hat with fake dreadlocks sewn into the outer rim. He laughed as he tossed it on my lap.

"What the hell's this?" I asked. A brief laugh eased my jumping stomach as I tried on my disguise.

"Here," Steve interrupted my laugh as he handed me a pair of sunglasses and a fake mustache. "Great costume," he confirmed as he eyed me.

"Who the hell am I supposed to be? Marley Wonder?" I exclaimed as I examined myself in disguise. Steve continued digging in the book bag and removed a long blond wig. The strong high made us laugh simultaneously as he put the wig on under a black mask.

"Let's go," he said. The words I dreaded had been brought to fruition and there was no going back. "Leave the car running," he bossed.

"I am," I answered as I quickly removed my hand from the ignition switch. We scurried into the building and rushed to the third floor. Loud music could be heard through the walls.

"When you knock, say 'Chris's friend' when she looks through the peephole. She won't suspect ya long hair and glasses are a disguise," Steve briefed me again as he withdrew the .380. "Go ahead!" he ordered. I knocked two times and banged three more.

"Who is it?" a white male's voice asked.

"Chris's friend," I mumbled and the sound of the door opening made me close my eyes.

"Come on in," the white boy said.

Steve bumrushed past me, nearly knocking my shades off. "Everyfuckinbody lay on the floor before I shoot!" Steve screamed. The loud music was our ally, for no neighbors would be able to hear the intrusion. Steve stormed over to "Chris."

"Gimme all your fucking money—now!"

"They got it," he stammered, trying to sound scared. Three lines of cocaine lay neatly on a nearby CD case. The white girl lay motionless on the floor. Two other white guys with long hair squirmed under the table.

"Move again and I'll kill you," I said, sounding more sarcastic than I preferred. "I want the money, weed, and everything else you got in here." *Shit! Hold on,* I thought to myself, *the pager had said there were four people.* Suddenly a loud *kabodge*! rang out through the apartment as a small black kid appeared outta nowhere. Three loud pops discharged from the .380. The kid fell helplessly as the hollow-points ripped into his chest. I heard a loud crack as the soft-nosed bullets shattered his sternum.

"Sonny!" the white bitch yelled as I just stood there, frozen into oblivion. This could not be happening.

Steve aimed the gun like a trained sniper in the combat position. "Pistol! Get up and grab that shotgun!" he ordered him, but Pistol lay motionless, blood gushing out of his nose, ears, and mouth. The shotgun blast had ripped into his leather jacket, and white fragments showed vaguely, resembling a crushed vertebra. The unexpected assault had startled everyone, and Pistol, with his back to the door, didn't have a chance. Pistol could be remembered pointing toward the back, but in the confusion he was ignored until it was too late. It all happened so fast.

"Get him up," Steve ordered me as I moved like a terrified robot. "We ain't leavin' without him," he said, as if I would have some objection. "Now give us the shit or all ya'll will be killed."

I looked over at Sonny; his frail chest didn't stand a chance against those hollow-tips, and my stomach felt sick as I thought of loading those bullets into the gun. I grabbed the shotgun to avoid any more surprises, and my brief attempt to pick up Pistol had soaked my shirt like perspiration. The back room was full of paraphernalia—scales and cut used for scrambled heroin. Sonny had been in the back, weighing out the supposed pound, and the money lay innocently on the dresser.

"Yo, she said look in the bottom drawer," I heard Steve yelling at me. With a slight tug, I opened the drawer. Big-faced fifties and one-hundreds stared back at me, neatly stacked with 1000 taped to each of them. There were eight stacks.

"Where's the weed?" I yelled back. "Ask the bitch about the weed."

"Under the bed," I could hear her crying.

I searched and found two trash bags, full of ganja, laying slightly open. To my surprise, a bag of high-grad heroin lay inside the trash bag, and my mind went back to the white lines on the CD case. That must've been dope; I remembered that I had mistaken it for cocaine. I wanted to call for Steve to show him the Desert Eagle .45 that lay on the nightstand and the heroin.

"Hurry up nigga!" he yelled, and the thought of him killing the white dudes filled me with terror.

"What if he's lost his mind?" I asked myself as I tied up the trash bags and placed the dope, gun, and money into the book bag I had brought along.

When I returned to the living room, everyone was tied up. The white girl had passed out from fear, I suspected, and a stench of feces reeked from her capri pants. The two white dudes looked like zombies—the combination of good dope and the front-row seats to two cold-blooded killings. Steve, who stood six feet three inches and weighed two-hundred fifty pounds, carried Pistol on his shoulder like a doll. The gun had been tucked into his waist. We had been there ten minutes.

"Let's go," he said to me, as if I needed an invite. As we exited the apartment, the distant sound of a fire engine could be heard. I prayed they weren't responding to a call from Southwoods. A cruel thought of ruining my seats flashed in my mind as Steve anchored Pistol's bloody corpse in the back seat. I loaded the trunk with the two trash bags, which must have weighed ten pounds each, and threw in the bookbag. I regretted leaving the shotgun, then remembered that it was used to kill Pistol. I skidded off as tears began to stream down my face, recalling the most dramatic fifteen minutes of my life.

"I didn't mean to, Shorty, but he would've killed both of us. Did you see that chopper that nigga had? We would both be dead right now, nigga, so stop cryin'. Fuck that nigga, man, fuck him," Steve said.

"I thought he was white," I numbly said.

"Me too. Fuck 'em!" he said with more conviction as we turned onto 702. Police cars began to flash by us by the dozens. *We're going to jail*, I thought to myself as I sped.

"Take him to my garage. I'll have the cleaner get rid of him in the morning." Steve told me.

We arrived quicker than expected, thanks to me doing ninety miles per hour the whole way. As we sat on the floor of his basement, Steve turned to me, puzzled, and for the first time he asked me, "What was in those bags?"

"Weed, money, and dope," I responded, lighting a Dutch Master.

"Oh," he said coldly.

Chapter 3

I awoke at 4:30 A.M. to what I thought was an apparent scream for help. I looked about frantically, only to find pitch-black darkness and the sound of Steve snoring peacefully. I looked at the pitch-black ceiling and a vision of Pistol's torn-open back made me cringe. I was having nightmares.

Pistol was still slumped over in my back seat, the body starting to decompose, and the garage reeked with death. It was the type of odor that I wish I coulda slept through. Steven's bedroom was in the basement, and with clever architecture, it connected to the garage. *I wonder if he has any blunts,* I thought to myself; I realized my chances of getting back to sleep were slim. Steve had told me stay in the garage, that he didn't want any blood tracked through the house, but I needed to get high; the constant screams, added to the reminder of a corpse in my car, were beginning to play on my mind.

I undressed myself down to my underwear and began feeling for the door that led to Steve's room. I must have bumped into fifty things before I found the knob. Great! It was open. I found the well-kept bedroom with pictures of naked women, and they greeted me as I flipped on the light. How could someone who lives with such religious parents have so much porn out in open view? I wondered to myself. I began looking through his dresser drawers like a cat burglar looking for jewelry. Then I found it: a half pack of Garcia Vega Barons. Not Dutch Masters, but they would definitely do.

The cigars were as stale as forgotten crackers, a testament to Steve's preferred Dutches. They needed careful precision; the least mistake and they would crumble to pieces. I removed both cigars and soaked them with my saliva. The aftertaste caused me to spit off my tongue. Shit, I needed a razor for my thumbs would create too much pressure and possibly crack the Vegas. I began my incision with finesse and finished the first one easily, which caused me to get cocky with the

13

second one. It exploded in my hands. "Fuck!" I exclaimed as a small pile of brown tobacco covered the cream-covered carpet. *Well, at least I got one and a half,* I reasoned as I tidied up the mess as quickly as possible and headed out of Steve's room. So excited about the discovery and what was about to happen, I almost forgot to turn off the light.

I sheltered the papers like an injured bird, using a cupping position as I fumbled back through the hallway. "The things we do to smoke these days," I laughed to myself. The thought of being high made me tingle with delight. I stepped over Steve and headed toward the trunk of my car. Although the windows were sealed, the odor was unbearable. The shadow of Pistol's slumped-over body showed through the tinted windows. I began to feel bad. For some reason, I hadn't liked this guy, and now he lay dead in my backseat. I remembered not inviting him into my apartment and questioning his heart. It was quite possible that Pistol had saved my life. I hated myself for misjudging him and taking his existence for granted. A tear fought through my resistance and leaked out of the corner of my eye. "Sleep well, dawg," I blurted, staring at the immobile shadow.

I let out my breath and took in some more as I popped the trunk. The words "sleep well" left a lump the size of coal in my throat. The trunk flew open, the ounce of blow stared at me curiously. *Maybe I should sniff a little to ease my pain,* I pondered. It was a mental checkup to see if I had completely lost my mind. "Yeah, right," I said aloud, and it enlightened me to see that I still had some good sense left.

I opened a trash bag and began filling my dark brown papers with the dark green substance. The brief mourning I had done over Pistol had caused the papers to dry and become brittle. I rolled fast and with expertise. The trunk light aided me tremendously and within three minutes, I had crafted two ugly ducklings (a term we use to describe badly rolled blunts). The odor quickly overwhelmed me and forced me to gag. Tears streamed down my face as I struggled to regain my wits. *Matches? In my pants,* I mentally answered my own question and searched the floor for my discarded jeans.

Found 'em. Yes! I searched for the matches and the garage lit up briefly as I struck one. I pulled hard on the blunt, as I noticed there were only four matches left. The weed burned stubbornly, so I lit another match and inhaled repeatedly until a bright red cherry showed.

I relaxed against the wall of the garage, and the gray smoke disappeared into the blackness of the garage. I kept the half a piece close by, fearing I would lose it. The weed soothed me; it made me happy to know that after what I had been through, I was still sane. I had never seen any murders at close range, never seen blood decorate a wall like that, and I'd never smelled burnt flesh from the invasion of hot slugs before. I could remember smoke coming out of Sonny's chest after he went into convulsions. I remembered the energy he put into his last breath as his chest blew up and then deflated one last time.

It had all been too much to bear. I began resenting myself for subjecting my psyche to such a rigorous and tortuous test. "It all could've been avoided," I stammered to myself in the dark. "It all could've been avoided," I said again as I pulled deeply on the Vega. A dizzy sensation intruded my senses and I became nauseated. Was the weed laced or was it the fumes of the garage mixed with decomposition? I wondered to myself as my eyes became heavy and I drifted into a coma. . . .

Chapter 4

Steve woke around 7:30 A.M.; he noticed me slumped over and snoring and decided not to wake me immediately.

"This nigga know I ain't supposed to smoke in my house!" he yelled angrily when he saw the piece of cigar lying next to me. "God damn! I gotta get this body outta here; dis nigga is rottin'!" he exclaimed when he realized the odor. He gabbed the piece of cigar that lay next to me. "Fuck it! Mom and Dad won't be home until Friday," and he used the last two matches I had left.

"I wonder what time the cleaner dude will open up," he said, half to himself. Steve knew all types of crooked businessmen. He knew crooked cops, drug smoking lawyers, and even an insurance adjuster who made fraudulent claims, given the right price. But none were more important than Mr. Porter was. The man had inherited his family's funeral home business more that thirty years ago. When business was slow, he began doing cremations for the mafia to make ends meet until business picked up again. Wives who killed their husbands, drug deals gone bad, any type of unexpected murder could be covered up for the small fee of $3500. Mr. Porter rarely did funerals anymore, but he kept the namesake for a front.

Rumor was that Steve did a robbery with Mr. Porter's nephew Joey, who accidentally shot a man while pistol-whipping him. Joey introduced Steve to his uncle, who allegedly threatened to kill him if his business practices were leaked. The way Steve tells it, he returned the same threat to Mr. Porter about his involvement with the murdered man and the two became instant friends.

Steve removed four thousand of the ill-gotten dollars and walked outside to use a pay phone to call Mr. Porter. He was worried about traces. Luckily, Mr. Porter was in, which meant someone had made an appointment.

"Hey, Mr. P. It's nephew Sti," he said into the phone when Mr. Porter came on the line.

"Hey nephew," Mr. P. said excitedly. "I though you were staying outta trouble. Goin' to college wit' all dem white folks in Pennsylvania."

"Delaware," Steve corrected. "Listen, it's not what you think. He one of my own. Just trying to disconnect the link, you feel me?" Steve tried to explain to Mr. Porter.

"Don't say too much, nephew. God damn! Them bugs got access to every phone line in the world, and you just a yappin' away!" he reprimanded Steve. "Be here in two hours so I can fix ya bike for ya, nephew. And don't forget I need three dollars and fifty cents for patches and glue." The phone went dead.

A wave of relief washed over his body. Pistol was a vital link to the murder. Once that link was severed, Steve could return to Delaware and resume his higher education. Pistol was failing anyway; everyone would think he'd said, "Fuck it," and went back to Georgia. His roommates couldn't stand him, and would be happy to know he had disappeared, he cleverly reasoned.

"I'm so glad nobody saw us leave except for May Jo, the white bitch who gave us a ride to Maryland. Oh well, I'll tell her that we split ways after we got back to school." He laughed to himself at the marvelous plan.

He immediately flagged down a hacker, looking for an early morning fix. "Take me to Eastern and Fifth," he ordered the driver.

"I need money up front, man," the toothless junkie explained to Steve. Steve flipped him a twenty dollar bill and reminded him, "Man, you know this only a ten dollar ride."

"Thank your very much," said the driver, and he pulled away from the curb.

" I gave you twenty because I want you to wait for me, then drop me off at those pay phones where you picked me up," Steve further explained. The driver then realized that this young boy was planning on getting his money's worth.

"All right," he reluctantly said, "but, son, could you hurry it up? I am starting to feel sick."

Steve ignored him. He was too busy thinking about how he was going to get Pistol to Mr. P.'s. Driving the same car that was used for the robbery and unexpected murders seemed risky, but the fewer people involved, the better. He looked at the dope fiend behind the wheel and thought, *Maybe we could use his car and just give him a couple of grams or raw and promise to only be gone an hour. Nah,* he decided as he pictured the odor permeating the interior of the raggedy Ford Taurus, *better to stick to the basics.*

"Here we are, Fifth. Remember not to take so long," The driver said as he switched off the ignition and reclined his seat. Steve stepped out of the car. He was so glad that he had taken off his shirt because Mr. Porter would flip if he had come walking into his place with a bloodstained shirt.

The old man was surprised. "I thought I told you two hours, nephew."

"I know, but I had the money on me and I was close by" Steven explained.

"Well, that's understandable," Mr. Porter laughed, revealing flawless dentures. "Can't argue with that, huh? So what happen, son? What happened?" he asked Steve.

"Man, we did a sting with only. . . ." but Steve cut himself off as he realized how foolish it had been to take only one gun to immobilize a house full of people. But there was no sense in lying to Mr. P. "One gun," he continued, "and the son of a bitch came out shooting through the door with a shotgun."

"You fool!" Mr. P. said honestly. "You know the rule." (3 niggas = 3 guns.) "And dis nigga who died didn't have no piece, did he?" Mr. Porter questioned.

"Well, the one died, but I shot the muthafucka before he could kill my man," Steve tried to save face.

"Where's the other dead nigga?" Mr. Porter asked, always thinking about the prospect of more business.

"We left him at the apartment. My man had the loot from the heist and I had my man," Steve explained to him.

"Okay, okay. Well, did you make out on the damn thing?" Mr. Porter wanted to know.

"Yeah, we got like fifty pounds of weed, ten grand, four guns, and mad grams of dope," Steve exaggerated slightly.

"Wowee. And only two niggas died. Shit, I reckon you did make out, nephew. I'll need two days before I heat up the incinerator. I'll keep the body until then for another thousand." Steve was being gamed outta too much cash, for he had made the mistake of revealing too much about the prize money, but he needed Porter and a thousand dollars was not going to stop him.

"All right, but I only brought $3500. I'll drop the rest off wit' the body," Steve said.

"Well, go get it then. I'll be here waiting," Mr. P. suggested as he had already forgotten about the two hours he had told Steve earlier.

"Bet. I'll he right back," Steve said and turned around and left the building, suddenly remembering the dope fiend's plea for a fix. He rushed out to the parking lot. But the hacker was long gone.

"Never pay a dope head up front, you front, you dumbass," he cursed himself. "Well, I still got money. I guess I'll take a cab," he said to himself while standing bewildered in the empty parking lot.

Suddenly, his pager sounded and he looked at the display.

"Shit! Cream's awake," he said to himself.

* * *

I awoke to an empty garage and a thumping headache. *I sure am glad I have some-thing to smoke,* I thought to myself as I patted the area surrounding me, knowing I'd left the weed within arm's reach. I couldn't find it right away and looked down, refusing to believe the inevitable until the evidence smacked the shit outta me. The empty pack of matches lay ten feet from where I'd left it after I had dozed off last night. That muthafucka smoked my weed! So I stumbled to his room and paged him, putting in multiple 911s and my code, 333. *The muthafucka must've lost his mind to smoke my weed,* I thought. Then I remembered the abundance of weed secured safely in the truck.

The phone rang and I decided to take a soft and lean approach with Steve. "Yo nigga, I see your turned into the weed bandit. Where you at?"

"Yo, I'm at the cleaners. I need some clothes pressed," he responded. The rotten smell of Pistol confused me. *He must've forgot the clothes,* I thought to myself. "Yo, I need a favor from you. I need you to bring your car for a tune-up. The mechanic's in." It was code talk. He really said for me to bring Pistol to Mr. P.'s to be disposed of.

"Man, nah, boss, I can't bear the. . . ." I cut myself off as I remembered our code. "I need you to come home," I said to him seriously. "I can't drive without air fresheners, and I need you to bring a pack of Dutches," I told him. What I really wanted to say was, "Nigga, you think I'm a take a chance on getting caught wit' this body by myself, man you must be crazy."

"Yo, the man waiting," he pleaded.

"So? You're not putting me in no trick bag, my man. We do'in this one together," I said coldly to him as I hung up the phone. The phone immediately rang back, but I didn't answer it. I chose instead to raid his refrigerator in search of some orange juice to cure my headache.

Steve arrived about an hour later and he had a peculiar look on his face. I could tell he was upset.

"Yo. I thought I told you not to track blood through my house," he said accusingly at me.

"I didn't," I defended myself, waving my feet in the air at him. "Man, hold up. You think I'm a stay in the garage with that smell? Nigga, you're crazy. Last night, it stank so bad I became nauseated and passed the fuck out," I told him.

"Yeah, I know, it was pretty bad," he admitted.

"Did you get those Dutches, man?" I asked him hopefully.

"Naw, I got a half a pack of Vegas in my room," He told me. It was now or never.

"Well, not really. See, I couldn't sleep last night, and I remembered you mentioned something about Vegas in your room," I lied. "So I kinda found them and smoked myself to sleep. But I didn't track nothing. Actually, I was naked."

Steve frowned and rolled his eyes. If it hadn't been for a thirteen-year-long friendship. He probably would've said I stole them. He couldn't do anything, though, except display a look of displeasure.

"Let's roll up and out," I suggested to him to take some tension out of the air.

He smiled up at me and said, "We're in over our heads, little brotha."

"I know, but it's no time to turn back now. We gotta get this nigga's blood off our hands," I said to him.

"Yo, I don't think I could go through this shit with anyone else. Let's take this to our grave, " he said weirdly to me.

"Yo, Stevey, no time for sentimental shit; let's just get this nigga outta my car before we're in jail to our grave," I said bluntly to him.

19

"You drive!" I shouted to him first and threw him the keys. Steve only lived about fifteen minutes from Mr. Porter's parlor, so the risk was minimal.

We started to the garage and were body slammed with the odor as we entered. The first step of death was the body fluids breaking down. A rotten smell of feces and meat filled the capacity of the garage.

"Yo, we won't be able to get into the car without a mask or something," Steve pointed out. We ended up spraying soaking wet towels with cologne and wrapping them around our noses and mouths.

We fought the odor as the car started without hesitation. Steve wound down the windows and opened the sunroof as we pulled out onto the street.

"We look stupid with these towels on our faces," I remarked to Steve.

"Yeah, well. We'll look even more stupid if we get pulled over, now won't we?" Steve said smartly as he noticed a police cruiser in the left lane attempting a U turn as we were turning right in the opposite lane.

"Shit! He's going to be right behind us if we turn," I said to Steve as sweat began to roll down my back.

"Should I turn?" Steve asked, putting our future on my shoulders.

"Well, if you don't, they'll be beeping up a storm and that will draw attention to us. Just hesitate a little," I suggested.

The cop car was frozen in the turning lane, but as soon as we decided to try it, I saw the green arrow flash and the cruiser U-turned directly behind us.

"Just be cool, Mo, we're fine," I assured Steve.

"What if he noticed the towels? Should I break on him or what?" Steve worriedly asked me.

"No. Just turn left on this next corner," I told him.

Suddenly the cop's lights turned on and my mind went blank. I couldn't even talk. We were going to jail.

"What do I do?" Steve asked me. He was beginning to jerk the gas pedal nervously.

"Fuck it. Pull over," I said to him.

"No!"

"Yes! We didn't kill Pistol," I reminded him.

Slowly, Steve began to pull over, tears of fear streaming down his face and flowing down the already soaked towel. The cruiser sped past us, ran a red light, and kept on his way. I almost had a heart attack. Steve stayed off of the road as we both softly cried a prayer of thanks. We had been two seconds away from a high-speed chase because of our guilt. The cruiser would've had no choice but to pursue our suspicious actions.

When we pulled into the funeral parlor, there was a brand-new-looking hearse double parked—a testament to it's lack of use. Steve ran inside, still visibly shaken by the events that had just taken place. He returned moments later.

"He said pull into the garage," and he began backing the car into the bay. I could feel a thousand pounds of weights being lifted off my chest.

Mr. Porter was standing inside next to an older version of the hearse parked outside. "All right. That's close enough. Come on outta there," he said to Steve.

He was dressed in preparation of his job. A rubber body suit covered his entire body and he had some sort of plastic device covering his face. Thick latex gloves were doubled up on his hands.

I jumped out of the car, not speaking to anyone, and ran to the wastebasket. Vomit shot outta my mouth like I was possessed. Steve was close behind me, and I could hear Mr. Porter's distance laughter as he spoke through the mask.

"Ya'll boys go on around front wit' ya weak stomach asses. I been smelling this shit for thirty-five years and never carried on like ya'll doin'," he continued to snicker himself.

I went out front; my stomach felt like a ball of hot acid. The upbringing had busted the vessels in my eyes. I went and sat in the lobby. The place was beautifully decorated.

Within minutes Mr. Porter emerged from the back, only removing his face shield to speak clearly.

"Ya know rules, nephew," he said.

"No, sir, I don't," I said dumbly to him.

"If this gets out, you'll die, you hear me? Now where is my thousand dollars?" he said sternly.

"What thousand?" I asked him.

"The thousand you owe me to get all that blood and shit out ya car, son. This is an expensive business, ya know?"

"Steve hasn't paid you yet?" I asked, still not getting it.

"Son, I need one thousand dollars. You and nephew can work that out later," he said to me.

" Well, it's in the car. The trunk, I mean," I told him.

"Son, this ain't no drug storage—unless we work something out, of course," he said greedily to me.

Finally Steve came back, his face all red and puffy, and it was obvious that he had been crying. I was relieved that Mr. Porter was his people because the man was giving me the creeps.

"Yo, how much we owe?" I questioned Steve.

"A thousand," the old man answered as if I had just questioned his honesty and integrity.

"Yeah," Steve agreed.

"Well, it's in the trunk with all the rest of the stuff."
Like I said, this ain't no free drug storage." The old man was obviously agitated.

"Okay. How much to hold everything except the dope? We can move that in two days," Steve asked him.

"For all that stuff you said earlier? Five hundred dollars a day, nephew. That cool?" He asked. It was not cool, but we had no other choice.

"Okay, fuck it. But we need something to drive for the time being," he said to Mr. Porter.

"Son, you ain't at Enterprise. My hearse is off limits, so that sounds like your problem, nephew. See? This is why I don't do business with Joey's friends," he exploded. "Ya'll little bastards want the whole world to cater to ya'll cuz ya'll spend

21

a coupla thousand. Hold dese drugs, give us a car, feed us, clothe us!' Mr. Cenavelli gives me ten grand, and a half the people he brings me are already chopped up." Mr. Porter was getting pissed.

"You're right, Mr. P., I apologize. Call us when the car is ready," Steve said to him. Then he went into the back and returned with the dope and two thousand.

"Now, fellas, I got work to do," Mr. P. said and motioned us out the door. *This guy is tough,* I said to myself.

Chapter 5

It changed from a routine noise complaint to an immediate backup plea after the first patrolman on the scene entered the lobby and saw the drops of blood leading from the upstairs. The trail led right up to the apartment that stemmed the loud music complaint, and frankly, Officer Simmons was scared to enter alone.

"Dispatch, we have an apparent injury, possibly a homicide, at the designated location," he radioed the precinct. Within minutes the parking lot was flooded with patrol cars.

After the typical three bangs on the door, the tactical team kicked it in and found three hostages tied up. The woman was crying for her mother, showing obvious signs of schizophrenia; the two brothers had somehow managed to reach the dope on the coffee table and lay in a nod next to the dead corpse. The rope that bound them was not even enough to keep them from getting high. Sonny's eyes stared at the ceiling, his stiff body covered in dried and coagulated blood. The officers on the scene radioed the detectives without touching a thing.

"You boys don't touch anything. We'll let Homicide handle this one," A fat policeman ordered the crew.

Within minutes a husky woman and two slender men arrived at the murder scene. No one could explain the trail of blood flowing down the stairs, and no one could decide where the blood had originated.

"Possibly another victim. We suspect he/she was taken with the apparent assailants, haven't talked to the victims yet," the fat cop briefed the lead detective, a Susan Taylor.

"Thank you, guys. We'll take it from here," the slender, light-skinned detective named Henry Bunning said and immediately called for a crime scene unit. "And we need a meat wagon and three ambulances," he said callously.

Detective Sue Taylor united the two men, which broke their nod. "Hi there," she said sarcastically. "Hate to ruin your high, but we need you'se to answer a lot of questions."

"Dem fucking niggers killed my friend," the older of the brothers blurted out. "My name is Ronnie Finx and this is my little brother, Harold. We came to buy some dope from that guy," and pointed to Sonny, "and that's his girlfriend, Landra. All of a sudden two niggers bust in, shootin' up the place," Ronnie volunteered, his sentences running together.

Finally Harold spoke for the first time. "You're forgetting about that guy Chris."

The other white detective, John Wollen, interrupted him, "Hold on, guys. One at a time, ya'll just start over and take your time."

Detective Taylor took over. "We'll ask simple questions; just try not to leave out any details." As they listened to the older brother explain the situation, Detective Bunning was checking the condition of the female. He fitted the latex gloves carefully as he removed her gag and rope. A smell of feces attacked him as he stooped toward the frightened girl.

"Sir, can you call my mommy and tell her I made a boo boo?" She laughed crazily and her eyes had a lost direction about them. The sight of her dead finacé and the thought of her own near death made her delirious.

"Girl's a little shaken up. With a little psychiatric care, she should be fine in a few days," Bunning reported. "Now, sweetheart, you're okay. I just need you to stay still until Mommy comes," he gently told her.

"Hey, detective, come look at this," someone yelled from the back. "This guy had a drug lab back here."

Detective Wollen jumped up when he heard "drugs." He suspected that was the cause of robbery. "I'll be damned," he murmured when the officer pointed to the .12 gauge shotgun.

There were shifters, a triple beam, and a digital scale; five ounces of suspected cut, cases of vials, and two cartons of deer slugs. A pack of weed bags and a full clip to an unidentified gun lay under the pillows. Inside the closet there were two bulletproof vests and an unloaded street sweeper tucked under a stack of towels. The outline of a large object could be seen under a handful of clothes.

"What's this?" the detective asked himself as he removed the disguise of the clothes. A large fireproof safe greeted him; it was equipped with an electronic combination device to prevent conventional means of safe cracking, namely the stethoscope. It was bolted to the floor of the closet.

As Detective Wollen left the room, the medical examiners were zipping up the body.

"Hey, Taylor, this guy didn't live here. It's nothing but women's clothes and shoes in the room along with a couple guns, paraphernalia, and a large safe. I think this is his stash house," Detective Wollen concluded.

"The brothers say he was from Florida, say he only comes up once or twice a month with her." He pointed to Landra. "Say he stays for a week, sells dope and weed until he makes fifty grand or so, then disappears. The brothers were apparent customers for his new batch of dope, and it gets strange here. Some guy named Chris called, apparently wanting to buy weed. Three minutes after he gets here, he makes a phone call. Then some guys come in, staging a robbery," says Bunning. "Chris was involved. Sonny was in the back cutting dope, we suppose hears the ruckus, comes out shooting, hoping to hit the suspected robbers, but Chris catches the bullet. The guy kills Chris so the robbers kill him. Bang! Bang! Another guy—a suspected Jamaican," continues Bunning, "goes into the back, comes out with two trash bags. They tie up these, grab our friend Chris, and leave. What was in those trash bags?" he asks this to older brother.

"Sonny was moving a lot of weed in the area, so I suspect marijuana," he replied.

"Were there any drugs found back there?" Bunning asked.

"Not in plain view, unless it's inside the safe," Wollen replied. "Take them to Homicide for finger printin'. Have them look at pictures of all local armed robbers and suspected drug dealers. She needs medical attention," Wollen ordered.

"And a diaper," added Bunning.

"We'll keep a close a eye on her," Wollen continued.

"They took Chris because he linked them to the crime. We'll still get them bastards," Taylor said forcefully. "I had some officers follow the trail; it leads to the rear parking lot, tire marks still fresh. We just missed the sons of bitches. Get some info on Chris and an analysis on the tread and see if we can figure out what type of car was used. Meanwhile, get a team in here for a more thorough search," she ordered.

"Can we go home? We didn't kill nobody," begged Harold.

"I know, but we need to take you guys for test and more questioning," interjected Wollen.

"That's what happens when you come to buy dope," Bunning teased.

As three officers rounded up the two brothers, an EMT was struggling to get Landra on the stretcher.

"You're not my mommy!" she screamed as they finally managed to strap her in. She looked a round, confused. "Where's my Sonny?"

The three homicide detectives stood in a small circle. The circus event had drawn a small crowd of neighbors, dressed in robes and with rollers in their hair, staring at the spectacle inside the apartment.

"Close the damned door!" Bunning said. An officer gently asked the crowd to step back as he closed the door behind him.

"All right. What do we got here?" Taylor began. "Some big-time drug lord comes in from Florida to Essex to sell grams of dope and trash bags full of weed. Somebody tipped the wrong crowd off and they were attacked. I had officers question everyone in the building, said they thought the apartment was empty until last week when the girl began blasting music. I showed a picture of this Sonny, and all they could say about him was he drove nice cars and spoke with manners. They said they only saw him a couple of times.

"I wonder how the dope fiend brother knows so much. . . ?" Bunning questioned. "Why would a guy with so much to lose tell these two burnouts everything, and why didn't this so called 'ruthless nigger,'" he was mocking the brother, "not kill the whole house?"

"Well, they say," Taylor defended, "that the guys threatened their lives and they probably only wanted the money. You don't go into an executional hit with one gun. I suspect it's some small-time punks that got in over their heads. They probably killed Sonny outta fear, and their friend may not be dead," she concluded.

"Call every hospital for an apparent gunshot wound," Wollen directed.

"Man, did you see those deer slugs?" Bunning disagreed about the fate of the missing gunshot victim. "My man, that's killing anything within ten feet. The ME says they found spinal fragments, and Sonny was shot here," he points to his chest and then to his back, "not here."

"Henry, we're speculating. We say the guy might not be dead," Wollen defended his theory.

"If he's alive, I want him," growled Taylor.

"Calm down, Suzy Q. I just wanna know how the brothers, who only see the guy once a month, can sit and explain the whole operation," said Bunning.

"Maybe Sonny was a nice guy. The neighbors even said he was. Nice guys confide in people. The older brother says he's been buying dope from Sonny for three years. It's not hard to—" Wollen argued.

"Bullshit," Bunning interrupted. "Nice guys don't blow out guys' backs and leave bone fragments scattered around. This fuckin' 'nice guy' had enough ammo to supply the whole apartment complex. Them brothers are in on the sting, I bet," Bunning assured.

"Maybe, but let's look inside Sonny's car; maybe it'll tell us something." Wollen would not be deterred.

The team of detectives walked to the door. As she passed an officer, she commanded, "No one comes past this tape without authorization."

It was a little after 2:30 A.M. and she was starting to become irritated. She hated working with Bunning. He was too fucking' brash for her liking. She was glad that the case was assigned to her, not him. It made her feel in control. She grabbed the keys to his 2001 Cadillac Deville rental car and headed down the stairs.

Bunning and Wollen were laughing peacefully when she met them at the car. She figured she was the brunt of whatever joke they were laughing at.

"What's so funny?" she asked them.

"Nothing," Bunning said and opened the door, "Mrs. Head of Investigation." Wollen smirked and Taylor rolled her eyes.

The interior of the car was immaculate, with a road map on the armrest. Taylor opened the glove compartment. A receipt for a one thousand dollar check that was made out to the car rental agency was discovered. It was dated from the third of March until the eighteenth. This was the eighth.

"I guess they were planning on leaving on the seventeenth," Taylor surmised as she looked at the paperwork. "The car was rented in Florida." She shifted through more papers in the car and there it was—a list with sixty names and numbers. "This must be his customer list," Taylor suspected as she scanned the names, which were in alphabetical order, looking for Chris. Chris T. was the fourteenth name on the list. An extension of 589 was next to his name. "This is our guy," she said and she continued to browse through the list until she found the names of the brothers and the same number.

"They must live with their parents," Wollen suggested as he looked over her shoulder.

To their mutual surprise, three names from the list immediately jumped out at them.

"Tommy Dain, Ricky Sunto, and Nina Porton. They're fuckin' cops!" all three said out loud.

"I worked with Dain and Sunto on a bank robbery last winter," Bunning recalled.

"And Porton's a dispatcher," added Wollen.

"This guy's death is going to roll a lot of heads," Taylor guessed. "So far, six people will lose their freedom or jobs."

"Eight," Bunning reminded her. "The two brothers."

Chapter 6

Within eight hours of leaving the body and the car with Mr. Porter, the car had become immaculate. The blood-dissolving solvent worked wonders, and fortunately it didn't discolor the upholstery. Mr. Porter used a unique shampoo to remove the odor from the car. After lightly scrubbing the shampoo with a special brush throughout the car, Mr. Porter used a hand vac to remove the soap residue after letting it set in for fifteen minutes. Free of charge, Mr. Porter had washed and waxed the entire car. A portable dryer was placed on the roof, the airflow being directed toward the floor. Actually, the upholstery looked much better than it did before the corpse was placed inside. The other trouble Mr. P. had faced was removing the splotches of blood that dotted the carpet floor. For that, he used a Teflon stain remover. After letting it sit for another eight minutes, Mr. P. used a steam cleaner on the deep scrubber setting. After continuous scrubbing, the camel-colored carpet looked better than ever. Accommodating his customer, he sprayed the car with a cherry-scented deodorizer that was so strong he became nauseated and dizzy. He rolled the two back windows down to neutralize the strong fragrance.

"It should be perfect by morning," he said to himself while inspecting his work. A look at his watch told him it was 9:30 P.M. "Well, shop's closed for the night," he figured. Thinking of the task that lay ahead, he said to himself, "Tomorrow I will heat up the incinerator and turn him into ashes. First thing," he said and laughed to himself about the two gullible young men whom he had told two days.

"Better yet, two hours," he chuckled to himself. "Them boys are so inexperienced, they can't even rob the dope man without shooting up the place." He continued to snicker to himself and shake his head.

Another quick glance at his watch and he pictured Joan. He reached for his Star Tec phone and hit the automated button. His home phone number appeared in a flash.

"Hi, baby, it's me. Look, we had to embalm three today so I'm running late. I'll see you at about ten to ten thirty," he lied to his wife. "Are the grandbabies sleeping okay?"

"Yeah, they sleeping good. Okay then, I'll see you in a little while," she answered, and he hung up.

Then he hit number two on his speed dial and the other line began to ring.

"Hey, sweets. It's Rudy," he said when the line was answered.

"Hi, handsome," the voice of a young woman said.

"Listen, I got an hour. I was wondering if I could come over for a little Moulin Rouge," he giggled at the last part.

"Sure, so long's you bring that cash, Daddy," she answered him. "Give me fifteen minutes," she said, and the phone went dead.

Mr. Porter loved call girls. He had three personally programmed into his phone. He never minded paying a couple hundred bucks for a few minutes of pleasure, as he pictured being tied up and whipped like a naughty child.

"This one's on you," he said to the body and turned out the lights and locked the door.

He walked a half a block north to his beat-up Cutlass Ciera. He never parked it at the parlor, always fearing the Mafia would wire it with explosives when they felt he knew too much. He thought about the 2000 Mercedes Benz he had just bought Joan on their fiftieth wedding anniversary, two weeks after she suspected him of having an affair.

Too late to drop her now, not after all these years, he thought as he gassed up the Oldsmobile and headed toward Tall Trees Village for an hour of sexual torture. . . .

I awoke a little after 8:30 P.M. to an array of phone calls. I jumped up, surprised to see nightfall, and ignored the ringing phone. *Damn*, I thought, *I dozed off at 1:00 P.M.*

Finally I answered the cacophony of rings. I paced around my apartment as I answered the call.

"Hey," I said into the phone.

"Well, hi dere. You're sure hard to catch up with too," I recognized Toni's voice.

"Hey, Ma."

"Where are you? Home? Well, I can't see you there," I smooth toned. Like I feared earlier, she mentioned me asking her to leave yesterday morning.

"I'm sorry, but I had twenty thousand dollars in here," I exaggerated, "and I was a little paranoid."

"Nigga, you stacked like that? Well then, let's furnish that lunch box of yours," she said, making a wisecrack about my small apartment.

"Let's go right now," I blurted out to her as I pictured the two thousand dollars.

"Nigga, it's damn near nine o'clock," she reminded me. That fast, I had forgotten how long I had slumbered.

"Come over, please," I begged her.

"I can't. I'm babysitting. Come over here though," she suggested.

29

"I don't got my ride. I let my mother take it to church," I lied terribly. "I'll get it back tomorrow morning. Look, I'll catch a cab over there, but I'll need your car for a minute," I told her.

"Nigga, come get it." Toni had become very accommodating since I mentioned the twenty grand. Before she wouldn't even let me hold the keys, now she's basically giving me the damn thing.

"Okay, I'll be there in a minute," I told her and hung up the phone and began scrolling through my pager. I had three sales waiting, and the thought of eliminating Sonny put a funny smirk on my face. I called all three, and like I thought, they were waiting patiently. I thought about Steve as I picked up the Ziploc baggie full of dope and placed it on the counter. He had left me with two thousand dollars and the dope and he trusted me with his cut of that. He had left me immediately after leaving the funeral parlor, saying he had a ride back to school. Outta the eight thousand, the greedy bastard Porter had six.

I removed my safe and threw the two G's in there, along with the $1375 I had made from sales before the caper. *Six thousand three hundred dollars and count - ing*, I thought to myself as I pictured the enormous amount of weed and dope we had stolen.

I grabbed the desired orders for my customers before rolling two humongous Dutches. I was becoming cocky and I knew it was just the beginning.

Within minutes of leaving, I flagged a hacker on Monravia Road.

"Take me to 126 Hanover," I told him and he pulled into the traffic. Church music played softly on the radio, which forced me to hesitate asking if I could fire up my Dutch. But soon enough, my mouth began to water and I thought about inhaling the smoke.

I handed him eight dollars and said quickly, "Can I blaze here?"

"For five more dollars," he told me in a businesslike tone. Shit, I had the money out and Dutch in position in two seconds flat.

We arrived at Toni's and I figured that the amount of weed I had rolled up could've sold for twenty dollars. Toni lived with her grandmother and she cracked the door. When she saw my obvious intoxication, she started bitchin'.

"Hell no. You not drivin' my shit all high," she told me.

I pulled out a hundred-dollar bill and slipped it though the crack of the door without speaking. She stopped in the middle of her sentence and handed me the keys.

"Just bring it back by nine o'clock tomorrow morning," she whispered. With her mood change suddenly she had put herself on front street; she acted like she could be bought, and an ugly side of her innocence was exposed. Christ.

I just grabbed the keys, jumped in the car, and pulled off. Jill Scott playing softly made the urge to smoke too great to ignore, so I fired up the second stogie. A few minutes later, Toni called.

"If you smoke, roll down the windows." She hated weed but the money made her forget her displeasure very fast.

"O-*kay*," I said to her and hung up.

After hitting up my three waiting customers, I received two more pages. I went through the routine process of going home, removing more weed, weighing it, and transporting it to the designated location.

After leaving my second customer, a seventeen-year-old Kingpin Mink, I received a 911 page from the payphone Fats usually called from. I called it back and gave my best performance as I listened to Fats explain how five people had run up on Sonny's pad and Sonny had killed four of them before being shot with a Desert Eagle. *The rumors people spread around these days are ridiculous*, I thought. Someone had decided to stretch the truth and make Sonny look like Tito Garcia.

"Damn, I can't believe that shit," I carried on.

"So I guess I'll have to start calling on you. You on?" Fats asked me.

"Naw," I lied. "Holla back at me tomorrow," I said to him and made sure I hung up on his fat ass first this time.

I arrived at Lodi Lounge around 11:30 P.M. Two for one was running until midnight and I was bound to catch some drunken freak who couldn't handle her liquor or keep me from the occasional free feel. DJ Wally gave me a shout out upon entering the club and the attention was just what I wanted.

"Free drinks for everyone," someone called out and I looked about the sparse crowd. I knew that everyone was half lushed and the round wouldn't cost that much, so I agreed. Two women, one white, one black, approached me as I positioned three big-faced hundreds in plain view, using them as a coaster.

"Baller come in here, trying to buy the bar out," the white girl remarked, impressed. "You wanna lil' fun tonight, Daddy?" A-ha! The word "Daddy" made me suspect hookers.

"How much?" I asked her.

"One hundred fifty dollars for both of us," the black girl answered.

"Let me have my drink in peace first. Meet me out front in fifteen minutes by the blue Geo Metro." Their eyes stared at me in disbelief, for they would've thought I had a big car with the way I was carrying on. "It's a customer's car, the T.L is on ice tonight," I bragged as I shrugged my shoulders. They agreed and disappeared, and I noticed the bartender was running in circles, trying to accommodate the free round of drinks for everyone I had bought. After fifteen minutes of this tiring escapade, an exhausted bartender approached me.

"Eighty, sir."

"Does that include yours?" I flirted with the bartender.

"No, I drink free," she said, unimpressed with me. She had probably seen it many times—a young kid, flashing one thousand's around. She'd seen the two-for-one trick before and wasn't fazed.

"Well, that's it then. You figured me out," I told her, trying to throw her off or at least get her to smile at me.

"Ten minutes left for the two-for-one. You're lucky," she said to me, and then finally, she smiled. I winked at her and slid a fresh one hundred across the counter and ordered another shot of Hennessey with a Sprite and told her to keep the change. She was clever; she knew I had already calculated my bar bill.

Like trained puppies, the two bitches stood leaning against the tiny car. My penis became aroused at the mere thought. I had never had two, and since along time ago, a *menage a trois* was my fantasy. I did a little two-step as I fumbled for the door key. The four doses of Henny had begun to run their course.

"Git in the front," I motioned to the black one. She was a chocolate girl, with a silky track. Her dark skin and sky blue eyeliner gave her an attractive tint. I lifted my seat and the other hooker bounded in.

"If I'd known this, I woulda brought the truck," I said to myself, but loud enough for them to hear, giving them the impression I had multiple vehicles.

After settling in, the black chick loosened my belt. "I began thinking singing a popular song by Noreiga. Getting Head in the Whip," I said and smiled undeniably. As my penis entered the warm confines of her mouth, I grabbed the ringing phone, thinking it was someone I could front to, but I had just missed the call. Then Toni's number popped up on my caller ID and I decided to turn the phone off for the evening.

After stopping for a pack of Dutches and a pint of cognac, I graced into the apartment. The two bitches stripped each other naked. The white girl had stretch marks on her breasts. I watched them indulge in a half a pill of dope before eating each other out, simultaneously. I sat back, stroking the Dutch and enjoying the show. I broke a smile; *I'm living like Fat Charles*, I said to myself.

After becoming so high I nearly passed out, I joined the party. They began double-teamin', suckin' my dick and my balls at the same time. A feeling of euphoria overcame me and I wanted to suck on the black girl's dark brown nipples, but after thinking of their profession, I licked them instead. I began to get really excited. The white girl mounted me and began bouncing on my meat with precise rhythm as I continued to fondle the soft set of breasts. Suddenly they switched positions, but I made the black girl get on all fours as I began to violently fuck her from the back. She begged for me to put it in her ass, and the white girl stood in front of her, rubbing her pink vagina all over the face of the black girl. I slowed down so they could regain control.

"Come over here and suck on my balls while I fuck her," I harshly ordered the white girl. As she stopped behind me and followed my orders, I resumed my reckless abandon in fucking the black girl.

I decided to have one more round with the experienced hookers. I fucked the white girl missionary style, then the black one from behind again. I felt myself retire after my penis refused to get hard again. The multiple ejaculations had worked like Nyquil, and I found I had trouble keeping my eyes open. I removed the one hundred fifty dollars from my stack and threw it toward the hookers, and I remembered them dressing as I sank into a deep, exhausted sleep.

I awoke to birds chirping and the sunshine glaring in. I was naked, with the exception of my socks and baseball cap. The large bulk of money felt uncomfortable pressed against the side of my leg, and I was glad it was still there. I was half hung over and realized that I hadn't seen the hookers out.

"Shit, them bitches coulda took me off . . . if I had anything of value to take," I joked as I sat up, half dizzy. My alarm clock lay close by and the time read 6:26

A.M. *Well, I guess I'll smoke a blunt, go to Toni's, and sleep 'til noon*, I thought to myself as I began to gather myself up.

I was glad that I had secured the weed after making my second round of sales last night. It was Tuesday and I was hoping the car would be ready by this afternoon. I transported the three thousand from the evening's hustle into the safe and removed a handful of weed to smoke, like my morning coffee.

As I pulled out the cheeba, I noticed my pager vibrating. It was my brother, Rock, who had been paging me since the wee hours of the morning. *Damn, I cut the phone off,* I remembered as I checked the other numbers.

Toni had paged me with a code of 69, which meant she wanted to fuck, or it was probably just a ploy to get her car back. I started to charge the phone and dialed my brother's number by heart. He answered groggily.

"Yo, what's up, my neezy? You hit me kind of early, I see. I was too busy getting fucked and sucked by two bitches," I bragged to him, eager to tell as many niggas as possible. "But anyway, I'm about to roll up and go over this other bitch house and crash," I continued, trying to sound like a true playa.

"Yo, I was calling because Steve said ya'll run across some raw dope. I wanna buy some and my shop opens in an hour," he informed me.

"Okay, good. I'll weigh you out a finger and be over in thirty minutes," I told him and hung up. I opened the safe, but the dope wasn't there. I checked my other stash spot, under my bed, and then the bathroom. Not there.

I started to backtrack my steps. "I came in, put it here, put the money in the safe, and got out the weed. Oh yeah, I left it. *I left it on the kitchen counter! Fuck!*" I yelled as I dashed to the kitchen. It was gone. So involved with the bitches, I had totally forgotten the dope was in plain sight. Also missing was the bottle of cognac I had bought but never cracked, more evidence of the apparent theft.

I ravaged the small apartment, checking places I didn't even use to store drugs. No dope.

"*No fuckin' dope!* Those bitches stole my dope—they stole my dope!" I screamed and cried and began to hyperventilate. My mistake had been dozing off before seeing them off. But only because I thought I had covered all corners. I had totally forgotten that I had put the dope in the kitchen, telling myself I would open the safe when I returned with the money. But I returned straight to them and totally forgot my responsibilities, and it had just cost me ten thousand dollars worth of raw heroin.

Chapter 7

As Detective Bunning sat at his desk, recalling the story of the two brothers, he was interrupted by his ringing phone.

"Bunning," he answered. It was Taylor and she had received the reports on Sonny's autopsy.

"His real name was Joseph Stewart and he was twenty-six years old. Cause of death was a crushed sternum and punctured and collapsed lung due to gunshot wounds to the chest," Taylor informed him. "ME says he had heroin in his system and his blood alcohol level was 0.9," she went on. "Bullets were hollow-tips, Talons, copkillers designed to puncture bulletproof vests. His chest was infested with bullet fragments. Have you found this Chris T. yet?" she went on to ask Bunning.

"The house is being watched and the phone number is disconnected. As soon as he comes home, we'll grab him. Wollen just released the brothers. He suggested we eliminate them as suspects, pending an interview with this Chris," Bunning offered.

"Okay, let's meet at the hospital at three o'clock. I hear Landra's doing well," Taylor said.

"Still on the psyche ward?" Bunning inquired.

"Yeah, but they say she's beginning to eat a little."

"10-4. Me and Wollen will run these prints and see you at three o'clock."

"Great," Taylor said and they hung up.

Detective Taylor began rethinking Bunning and their differences. She was now glad he was on this case, the man was a brilliant detective. She called the officer who ran the K-9 unit.

"Hi, this is Sue Taylor. What did we learn at the apartment?" she began when he came on the line.

"No more drugs were found; however, we managed to manipulate the lock on the safe and it contained fifty-five thousand dollars cash, all in hundreds," he reported to Taylor, conveniently forgetting to mention the ten thousand he had split with his partners at the discovery. "Gonzalez and Reyes witnessed me count it and seal it. It's on its way to the crime lab now for printing," he added to downplay any suspicion she might have. "Other than the cash, the place just had trace amounts of heroin and marijuana."

"Damn, fifty-five grand, huh? That's a lot of money," Taylor exclaimed. "Okay, thanks, Pete. I'll keep you posted and will call if I need you."

"Sure," Pete replied, happy with the realization he had just escaped with thirty-three hundred dollars for an hour's work. "Shit, he dead, he can't use it anymore," he rationalized to himself as he pictured his new motorcycle.

Taylor arrived at headquarters at a little after two o'clock and was surprised to learn that Bunning and Wollen had left, reacting to a call that Chris had been spotted entering his home. A small note was taped to her computer screen.

Why didn't they call me? she wondered angrily. *This is my fuckin' operation,* she cursed to herself. She grabbed her cup of coffee and left within minutes of arriving.

By the time she had arrived at the Towson location, Chris was sitting, startled and bewildered, in the back of a police cruiser. She scanned the team of police until she spotted Wollen and marched up to him.

"Why wasn't I contacted, John?" she asked.

"Sue, we reacted. Nobody's trying to steal your light; we know who's in charge," Wollen lightly said to her.

His comments made her soften. "You're right; we're all in this together. Has he been placed under arrest?" she asked, pointing to Chris.

"For what? We only advised him about the murder and told him we needed him to answer some questions at the station."

"Where's Bunning?" Taylor asked.

"Well, if he's not still interrogating the shit outta that poor man, then he's probably around here somewhere," Wollen answered her.

"Shit, I told hospital officials at Delfield Memorial that we'd be by there at three," she remembered.

"Well, she's not going anywhere. We'll get to her first thing in the morning. Right now, let's focus on what this Chris guy has to say. Taylor, we checked his entire body; the man doesn't have a scratch," Wollen said.

When they arrived at HQ, the team of detectives stood looking at the handsome guy through the two-way mirror. He had been pleading to the officers on the entire ride that he was being falsely accused of whatever had happened.

"You're not under arrest. Your name was thrown into a murder, and we just wanna ask you a few questions," the officer driving the transport cruiser had explained to him.

After intensive questioning, it was learned that Christopher Thompson used heroin intravenously and that he knew the brothers, Ron and Harold Finx. He had said that he had no idea that Sonny was in town, because he had been in New York for a month trying to get clean. He had a strong alibi—pictures from his family reunion in Syracuse that he had attended on the day of the murder.

"And he's never been shot," Taylor added.

Bunning restated his original theory. "Them brothers are in on this. If they know this guy, then who was at the apartment? Wouldn't they have said that the guy was impersonating Chris, that they knew what he looked like? Why would they act like their buddy got shot if they knew he was in New York? The brothers probably got the impostor to use his name. Sonny probably trusted their judgment enough to serve anyone they sent to him, so he probably had no idea what Chris even looked like," Bunning finished.

"Or too doped up to remember," Taylor added.

"The brothers' systems were loaded with heroin. Heroin leaves the system within seventy-two hours, so we know they were using right up until the murders. They were the inside source," Bunning concluded his theory.

"We've had that poor boy questioned for six hours. Release him before every lawyer in the city is crying for a civil suit," Taylor commanded.

It was exactly 9:00 P.M. Chris was thanked for his cooperation and then released.

"We got the report back from the lab," Taylor started. "The hair analysis indicated it came from an African-American, probably a male, which we already suspected. They were able to extract DNA from the blood sample, and so far we know it's xy, meaning male. We'll know more after the analysis is complete. The rest of what we know comes from eyewitness accounts: black male, late teens to early twenties, approximately six feet tall. We *need* to find that body," Taylor emphasized the obvious.

"We'll pressure those brothers until something comes up. Get authorization from brass for a wire tap and video surveillance. If those boys make one wrong move, we'll nail 'em," Bunning said while Wollen nodded his head in agreement.

Meanwhile, Mrs. Jenkins (the nurse at Delfield Memorial) was making her evening rounds on the psychiatric ward. She remembered Landra Dixon, the pretty young white woman who literally had been scared out of her mind. She was starting to come around, and the compassionate black nurse remarked, "I'm glad those police ain't come messing with that girl," as she entered room 407.

Landra's shadow could be seen in the bathroom and she could be heard crying softly. Mrs. Jenkins ran over to her, turned on the light to get a better view, and saw a small amount of blood dripping down Landra's leg, who was sitting on the toilet clutching her abdomen. Knowing that Landra was six weeks pregnant from the tests she had undergone upon her admission, she suspected a miscarriage.

"My baby. First Sonny and now my baby, oh please, God, no," Landra cried softly, confirming Mrs. Jenkins' fears.

Mrs. Jenkins hit the call button on the headboard of the hospital bed and then went back to attempt to console Landra. "Lanie, the doctors are coming as fast as they can. We are going to do everything we can to save your baby," she said softly, while stroking Landra's blond hair. When Landra looked up at her, Mrs.

Jenkins was able to see the amount of blood that had fallen into the toilet. Even though it was diluted, the experienced nurse could tell that this was serious. Within a few minutes, an Asian and an Indian doctor came storming into the room.

"Patient's having a miscarriage," Mrs. Jenkins informed them.

"My baby's gone," Lanie whispered as that lost look reappeared on her face.

The doctors moved fast, hoisting Lanie's nude body on a gurney and rushing her into surgery to stop the hemorrhaging and to perform an emergency D&C. Mrs. Jenkins collected the tissue that had fallen into the toilet for histology, and as she scooped up one glob of tissue, she imagined it was the baby. After the medical abortion, the D&C, where Lanie's uterus was scraped and the remaining fetal tissue vacuumed away, doctors declared Lanie okay and in good condition, but of course, the fetus had been lost.

"Stress," the Asian doctor suggested. "The girl was under too much anxiety to properly nurture the fetus and her body knew it." He referred to a spontaneous abortion, where the body rejects the embryo for no other apparent reason.

Lanie was given Tylox and was fast asleep. Her psychiatrists were worried that they had taken a backward step in Lanie's mental recuperation. Mrs. Jenkins was instructed to keep a close eye on Landra throughout the night.

"I'd like for you to check on her every hour, on the hour, and more if you can find the time," the lead psychiatrist ordered Mrs. Jenkins.

"Yessir," she complied obediently.

At precisely 3:00 A.M. Landra awoke to the nightmarish sound of Sonny's voice begging her to join him; IVs and tubes snaked from her arm and nose to a bag that stood beside her. She heard a noise and pretended to be asleep until Mrs. Jenkins had vanished back down the hallway. She untangled the tubes and ripped out her IVs and oxygen tube. She had decided to relieve her pain once and for all.

"I'm coming, Sonny. Here I come, baby. We're going to be a family again," she whispered as she untied her ankle restraints. She used all her energy and strength to climb up on the bed and tug the bedsheet off to tie firmly around her neck. She looked about for something to hang herself from and saw the propeller of the ceiling fan. She tied the other end around that and felt a tug as the sheet stretched to its limit. Tears began streaming down her face as she was again reminded of all that she had lost—that Sonny and their baby were dead.

"I won't go back to Florida without you, baby," she said. "Our Father, who art in Heaven, hallowed by they name. They Kingdom come, thy will be done, on Earth as it is in Heaven. Give us this day our daily bread and forgive us our trespasses, as we forgive those who have trespassed against us. Lead us not into temptation, but deliver us from evil, for thine is the power and the glory forever. Amen." With that, she stepped off the bed.

She choked as the homemade noose tightened its grip around her frail throat. She started wheezing for air as her throat was cut off. Finally, her fighting and instinctual struggling began to cease as her trachea and then her lungs collapsed. Urine and blood began running down her leg, dripping from her swaying foot like a leaky faucet.

Death had come for Landra Dixon.

Chapter 8

A look of disbelief played across my face as I sat there contemplating blowing my brains out.

I scolded myself out loud. "How could I forget about ten thousand dollars worth of dope? Has weed burned my brain cells to the point of mental retardation?" Oh God. What would I do? What would I tell Rock? What would I tell *Steve?*

As visions of Sonny's lifeless body haunted me, I looked over at the pack of Dutch Masters. I wanted to smoke badly but thought about its obvious affliction to my brain and memory. In the end, instinct won out.

Habitually, I removed the cellophane wrapper protecting the cigar as I began to think. It was now a little after seven and I knew my brother was waiting. I wanted to play a round of Russian Roulette—just to prove how miserable I was—but the thought of that same pistol being used in a murder only troubled me further.

My phone began ringing furiously and the ID indicated my brother's cell phone number. I decided to reveal my gaffe.

"Yo," I answered, mournful, totally south of my tone of our previous conversation. Rock didn't catch on.

"Donny, come on, man. I'm jammin' out here." The sound of my real name freaked me out and could only mean urgency. It had been quite awhile since he had reverted to my Christian name. Even my mother had started calling me Cream three years ago, and as a statement I had it tattooed on my left bicep.

"Listen, Robert." *Two can play the real name game,* I thought. I said, "The bitches I had in here last night stole all the dope. I had passed out due to an OD of Hennessy and four blunts to the head," I sheepishly tried to defend myself.

"Man, how do two freaks walk out your house with anything other than their panties? I thought I bought you a safe!" he chastised me. "You're so stupid fallin'

38

asleep like that before seein' those hookers out. Niggas get killed like that," he went on.

"Man, what am I going to tell Steve?" I worriedly asked, trying to play the scared little brother role.

"I don't know! All I know, asshole, is that I'm bout to lose out on seven to ten thousand dollars from my morning shift!" he barked. "I'm gone, man. I need to find some blow." He hung up on me before I could apologize.

I already felt bad enough and it was only strengthened by Rock's shakedown. His verbal beating only darkened my already cloudy mind. While listening to his outrage at my stupidity, I had begun to roll the Dutch and it was ready to be exercised by the time he rudely hung up on me.

I walked to the stove, hoping the dope would be sitting there but knowing it wouldn't be. A strong cloud of cannabis filled the kitchen as I thought about my life.

This lifestyle is killing me, I thought absently as I looked at the ugly cigar. Selling weed, smoking weed, robbing people, and fornicating with all kinds of different women—it was all disturbing my mental and physical health.

"I need to change," I said aloud to myself. I even strained a tear from my eye to convince myself of my own sincerity. I hoped and prayed something would change me.

I opened the safe while the cigar dangled from my tightened lips. I counted the stacks and stacks of money. I counted out five thousand dollars.

"I'll just tell Steve I sold all the dope," I said aloud as my mind changed, no longer interested in having a personal pity party.

Seeing my diminished cash flow, my stressful mood returned. I only had a few thousand left in the safe. I began inhaling deeper on the cigar, as if the faster buzz was depended upon.

I picked up my Nextel bill. It was well into the hundreds, this the result of having no home telephone. I called information and jotted down the number for Porter's Parlor. Then I called Toni.

"Good morning." Her feisty grandmother answered after the second ring.

"Good morning, ma'am. Is Toni awake?" I asked politely.

"No, young man, she's not. Who dis?"

"This is Donny, Mrs. Washington." I timidly answered her.

"Boy, if you don't bring dat girl car back, I'm a put my foot in yo ass!" Before I could try to plead my case, her line went dead.

I took a deep breath and hung up the phone. What a day! I stupidly reached for the pack of Dutches, telling myself I needed one for the road. I hoped Porter was finished, I wondered to myself as I undressed quickly. It was already 7:39 and I had just enough time for a dick and balls bath (that's what we called quick showers, where you only washed under your arms and your dick and balls). I was done by 7:45 and decided to dress casually in a short-sleeved, handmade Coogi sweater, which looked good with my tan, a pair of beige Chinos, and some beige Gucci loafers. I decided against socks; it was spring, after all. Being this damned depressed, the least I could do was dress nice.

I was haulin' ass to Toni's house, glancing at the blunt that lay peacefully on the passenger seat, when I saw a cop car dart out of nowhere, get in behind, and flash me the blue lights. Like an honest citizen, I pulled over immediately and removed my license from the Coach wallet my sister had given me on my birthday. Searching frantically for the registration, I noticed the cop still sitting in his cruiser. After locating the registration in the cluttered glove box, I realized with surprise that the car was registered to Toni's grandmother.

"Get out of the car with your fuckin' hands up!" The cop screamed from his window. Omigod. Two other patrol cars had pulled up while I was looking for the registration.

I did my best to stuff the blunt under the seat without being noticed and stepped out the car, with my hands up. My immaculate dress did not coincide with the cheap, compact car.

"Put your hands on the hood. Slowly," the one officer told me. I obeyed and noticed the other officer closing in on me with his service weapon drawn. They expertly patted me down and led me to the original officer's patrol car.

"Sit back here, son, while we sort this out," he told me.

"What did I do, sir?" I asked innocently.

"Some old lady reported this car stolen at 5 A.M. this morning."

"No, no, no, I date her granddaughter. We mutually agreed that I could hold the car until 9 A.M. today. See, I have the car keys," I explained.

"Just sit tight, sir," he told me while the other cop was examining the ignition switch and steering column and, to his surprise, removed a set of keys. The car door was slammed in my face and I was allowed a few minutes of peace to curse myself, the world, and everyone in it.

"Dear God, why did you wake me up today?" I prayed in vain. *This has got to be the worst day of my life*, I thought.

Minutes later, the Asian-looking cop came back to me and asked to see my license. Whew, I was relieved to see all they wanted to do was a routine license check. It had all been a misunderstanding.

"I'm handcuffed. Could you please take it out of my back pocket?" I innocently asked, my big eyes staring up at him. He did as asked and then shut the door again, leaving me to scrape my stomach from the bottom of my feet. After twenty minutes of waiting, I was starting to become a little restless. *Why are they still hold - ing me?* I asked myself. It was at that moment that I saw the paddy wagon pull up. What the fuck? The other officer marched over and yanked open my door.

"You have the right to remain silent. . . ." Too stunned to do anything else, I closed my eyes and refused to listen. Gripping the Dutch in his hand, he loudly began to recite my charges.

"Possession of stolen vehicle and possession of marijuana." Oh Jesus. A quick look at his nameplate told me his name was R. J. Sunto.

"Sir, please call the lady. This is all a big mistake. She didn't know I had borrowed the car until about twenty minutes ago, when I spoke with her on the phone, sir." I tried desperately to get someone to listen.

"You'll have to discuss that with the commissioner. She says you stole it. Now you get outta my car." As I was dragged to the waiting paddy wagon, I saw Sunto remove the ashtray and pour out the ashy remains of a small piece of blunt. My unlit Dutch he had gripped in his hand while reading me my rights had disappeared. That mothafucka was stealing my weed! And then charging me for it!

The driver of the wagon was a short bald man who looked like Michael Wilson. He opened the back door and I voluntarily hopped into the steel jail on wheels, which was already occupied by two winos and a young white kid, nodding. The large van was geared into drive and we accelerated jerkily, jolting everyone to the left, which broke the white boy's nod.

"You asshole," he muttered before nodding back off.

The smell emanating from the two winos was unbearable, and I vaguely wondered how they could tolerate it as I thought about the cop who stole my blunt. *I'm not going to forget that crooked bitch*, I vowed to myself as the van pulled up to the gates of the garage leading to the Central Booking Intake Center.

Because of my innocence, the thought of prison hadn't crossed my mind yet. Not until the van started backing in, giving off that ominous beep, did I become jittery. I had never been to prison before.

* * *

At 8:30 A.M., Mr. Porter arrived at his namesake. He reasoned that he would finish up and call the boys by twelve. The body had already been greased and prepared for cremation. Steve had also ordered Mr. P. to incinerate the brand new .380 that was used to kill Sonny, so Mr. Porter placed the gun inside the oven tray after it had already preheated to the designated two thousand degrees. After fifteen minutes, Mr. P. removed the gun from the tray and the once stainless .380 was reduced to a silvery liquid. Mr. P. was at a loss as to what to do with this liquid metal mess and decided to stash it under the body when he put that in the incinerator.

He used a specially designed spatula to evenly spread the mixture in the bottom of a tray before it cooled. He then put the half-frozen and greased body on top of it, and the fiery lava instantly began to cool. Mr. P. increased the temperature to two thousand five hundred degrees, slid in the body tray, slammed the door, and chuckled, "Give that turkey thirty to forty minutes and he'll be nothin' but an ashtray."

He exited the restricted area and yanked the thick rubber gloves off his wrinkled and gnarled hands. *I oughta give this illegal shit up*, he thought to himself. He had already made himself infamous throughout the underworld. He had two million in a money market, and here he was risking his life for four grand. *That's it! I'm done*, he declared at his business line began to ring.

"Porter's Parlor," he answered. On the other line was a grieving widow who had just lost her husband to the big C. He couldn't believe it. It had been three years since he had handled a legitimate funeral and the arrangements. While the lady explained her husband's last wishes, he suddenly felt as if he earlier thoughts had been a premonition. Upon hanging up with the poor old lady, Mr. Porter was a changed man.

"I want these drugs outta my parlor and I'll give those boys their five hundred back; they can store their dirt somewhere else," he declared as he called the number Cream had left for him on the notepad. He was hoping to hear Cream's voice, but instead he was left with his voicemail.

"Hey, nephew. I got an extra ticket to the ball game, if you're interested. Call me." He was a season ticket holder of the Baltimore Orioles, so if the call was being traced, it could be easily explained away.

After going to the Captains' for a crabcake lunch platter, he returned to his parlor and entered the restricted area. The autoclave was buzzing and the light was blinking, so the procedure was complete. Mr. Porter stared through the protective glass window while adjusting the oven to cooling mode. The body had been reduced to ashes, nothing more, and the once stainless .380 was a black stain on the tray. He removed the remains after the temperature had reached a safe level and made three trips to flush them all down the toilet. He then got a hose, one that was connected to a bottle of heavy-duty cleaning solvent, and thoroughly sprayed down the inside of the oven. The standing water was then shop-vacced up, which was also flushed down the toilet. To seal the deal, Mr. P. took a long piss, literally pissing away any evidence that could've been left behind.

As he washed his hands, both literally and figuratively, he thought about all the years he had spent with his now late father. "I'm done, Dad. You and Ma worked too hard for me to ruin your namesake. I'm done," he vowed.

Chapter 9

At 9:45 A.M. Detective Taylor was sipping her coffee and checking her email when her phone rang.

"Taylor," she answered. She listened for a moment and then said, "Oh my God, no, Dr. Mosaki. I am devastated; she was the central part of our investigation. . . . Well, I'm so sorry that happened under your care. . . . Well, we didn't come because something urgent popped up, but I was actually just about to call and schedule another appointment this morning." This was a lie. "I am sorry to hear about such a tragic ending; the girl had so much youth about her. . . . Okay, Doc. . . . Thanks. By the way, she didn't leave a suicide note, did she? . . . Okay, I understand. I hope you feel better, too. Goodbye," and she hung up the phone. She felt her investigation slowly slipping down the drain.

"Dammit, I needed you, Landra," she said aloud to no one in particular. She picked up the phone and hit two keys.

"Wollen, it's Taylor. Remember your comment about Dixon not going anywhere? Well, she did. She's gone. She committed suicide between 3:00 and 3:55 A.M. She was found by the nurse in charge who was assigned to look in on her every hour. Well," she gasped, "apparently, she had had a miscarriage yesterday evening, and what with everything else that happened and the side effects of the antidepressant they had her pumped full of, she just went over the edge, I guess," Taylor surmised. "What are we left with, John?"

"The brothers. They will, unfortunately, either make this case or break it. The crime lab says the prints match the four victims, so these robbers must've worn gloves. One strange discovery did pop up—strands of synthetic hair were found near the victim. I suspect the murderers wore wigs for disguises," Wollen guessed.

After a brief knock, Bunning burst in, a fresh cup of java in his hand.

"Mornin'. I contacted Mr. Thompson this morning after I heard about Dixon, and check this out—he said Sonny has never seen him before. Says every time he wants to cop heroin, he goes to the apartment and the brothers take his money into the back where Sonny shifts and weighs the dope. The brothers then return with the shit and he leaves. Says that Sonny never wanted to be seen," he concluded, pleased with himself.

"So 'Chris' could've been anyone," Detective Taylor said.

"Exactly. The brothers deal with all the customers."

"So what was Landra's role?" Taylor asked.

"To make sure the brothers didn't stash any money from Sonny. She was the supervisor," Bunning answered.

"So why did Sonny have a customer list?" Taylor wanted all the bases to be covered and wanted all the information.

"He's the man. The brothers probably made it out and Sonny just looked over it outta sheer curiosity to know who was going to be coming to his house for the next ten days."

"So the brothers know about Dain and Sunto?" Taylor asked.

"Obviously, they did all the wheelin and dealin'."

Taylor had quizzed Bunning like a pupil practicing for the national spelling bee, and Bunning, being a great student, had done all his homework.

"Great work!" Wollen shouted over the speakerphone. "I want those brothers under constant surveillance. Did we get a judge to sign off on the tap?"

"Yeah, but so far, nothing beneficial. All we know is their mom flirts with her boss late at night and they're supposed to fake overtime tomorrow and meet at the Marriott for a rendezvous of some sort. Captain only gave us seven more days of this, so I say question them again, this time with our new insight. Usually criminals crack when they realize someone's been spilling their hand," Bunning answered.

"And let's go right now before we find someone else dangling from a ceiling fan," Taylor said forcefully. "Wollen, meet us in the parking lot."

Upon reaching the brothers' house, Wollen and Taylor approached the front while Bunning surveyed the back, just to be on the safe side. A young woman was seen leaving and didn't notice Bunning in his plain clothes.

"Excuse me, miss, are Harold and Ron home?" he politely asked.

"Yeah, half dead until I brought them their gate shot. Who are you?" she asked after already talking too much.

"Just a friend, lookin' for a little snack," he lied. God, she was easy.

"Well, you're not gon' find any around here. Ever since that kid Sonny got smoked, dope's been scarce. Shit, I had to ride all the way down Pennsylvania and North just to keep from getting ill. Then I had to bring those assholes four pills of scramble just so they could get outta bed," she complained, giving Bunning much more than he had ever dreamed.

"Shit," Bunning acted depressed. This was too easy. "Guess I'll have to make a trip into town then," he said.

"You need some company? I could show you the hole," the girl advertised. This female fiend was trying to get a free high.

"Naw, but give me your number. I'll take us up tomorrow morning," he lied to her. She hurriedly wrote it down, with the feeling of just hitting a potential jackpot. Bunning needed someone like her—an inside source that talked so much she could send twenty people to prison. He decided to remain anonymous.

"Well, I gotta go . . . ," he looked down at the paper she had given him, "Jenny."

"See you tomorrow," she promised as she disappeared into the alley to retrieve her car.

Finally, after ten solid minutes of knocking, then banging, Ronnie stumbled to the door. The dope must have taken effect because he felt his muscles begin to come alive. He opened the door to see the detectives and wished he could have slammed it right back in their faces. But he couldn't.

"What's up?" he asked as innocently as he could.

"We need to ask you a series of questions," Taylor told him.

"I've already answered your questions, fat ass," Ronnie stupidly told Taylor.

"I know, but you see, your version has been challenged by another unknown source," Taylor explained, and as a look of unadulterated terror filled Ronnie's face, the detectives walked on in.

"Mr. Finx, we spoke with Chris Thompson. He never was at Sonny's that night and he's never been shot. You lied to us and we want to know why," Taylor asked him sternly.

"I didn't wanna tell you I pitched for Sonny because you woulda locked me up," Ronnie whined.

"So who was it?" Taylor's patience was wearing thin with this junkie. A blank look overcame his face as if he was trying to place a face with a name or just trying to think of another excuse. He stared at the wall as if it were talking to him.

"I can't remember," he lamely offered. "Harold! Get down here!" he shouted, trying to shift some of the weight off of him and load it onto his brother. Harold came hopping down the stairs jubilantly until he spotted the detectives gathered in his living room. His eyes almost popped out of his head.

"Who was that guy who came to buy the dope, shit, I mean weed?" Ronnie pointedly asked his brother.

"I don't know. Sonny knew him; he let him in," Harold noticeably lied.

"That's right!" Ron agreed.

"Why would Sonny shoot his friend?" Wollen asked the brothers.

"Listen, guys, you're lying so bad your ears are smoking. We can see and smell guilt. I'll tell you what; we'll leave, call up whoever put you up to this, and you tell him we're on his ass. We gave you assholes a break, but you're one cover-up away from being charged with murder. So you can take the fall, be my guest, I don't care. I just want this case to say solved. But someone's going to jail for these murders and it won't be us sittin' in prison screaming our innocence," Taylor threatened.

"Now listen. This guy told us you guys deal to cops and fifty-seven other people on a weekly basis. He informed us that you two do all the paperwork and distributing. That's fifteen years, fellas, no parole," Wollen warned. "Tell us your role or expect indictment papers in the mail," he promised.

The mention of cops as customers had hit them close to home. The brothers were certain someone was talking, and this terrified them so badly they seemed to emit an odor of fear.

* * *

After being booked, fingerprinted, and having my picture taken; and after I had been harassed about my sweater and shoes, I was thrown in a small holding cell with nine other black men. We were given bag lunches that contained a slimy piece of bologna, two cold slices of cheese stuck to four pieces of bread, an oatmeal cookie, an orange, and a grape drink with a polar bear riding the carton. Regulars, who knew what they were supposed to get in their bagged lunch, complained about their missing bags of chips. The guard—a fat and grotesque black woman with slept-on braids—suggested it would be a couple hours before seeing the commissioner and using the phones to inquire about the missing chips.

"That bitch been saying dat for hours now," a young kid with a ripped shirt and a black eye yelled.

"She probably gon' wait 'til shift change. She just wanna go home and eat all our chips," joked another black kid, this one with cornrows. Then he turned around and looked at me. "You a lawyer or sumthin', comin' in here with a Coogi on?" he asked me.

"Naw, Bo, I'm a hustla, nigga," I corrected him. "Dese bitches made a mistake talkin' 'bout I stole my girl car. Man, her grandmother don't like me 'cause Shorty spent the night at my house last week, then I put her out when I had to take care of business, so she went home and told her grandmother," I explained to these young'uns, needing someone to listen and feel my pain and frustration. "The fuckin' car in her grandmother name, and the bitch snuck me the keys last night so I could get my hustle on and then the grandmother reported the shit stolen," I continued. Then when I noticed I had an audience of eager listeners and I realized that people of all colors and ages like to hear other people's business, I stopped talking and just shrugged my expensively clad shoulders and sat on the bench with the rest of 'em.

"You goin' home. The commissioner gonna re-con that," a junked-out voice reassured me. I stuffed my empty brown bag with the juice carton to make a pillow and laid my head against the wall. My high was completely blown and I wanted to tell the audience about the crooked cop stealing my Dutch but feared I may have been looked at like a gabber who just liked to hear himself talk slick, so I didn't say anything about it. So I laid up, hoping someone else would take the stage. They did; it was the guy with the ripped shirt and the shiner.

His name was Leroy McCoy and he explained how he had beat the shit outta his girl for smoking his coke and then attacked the police after she had had somehow managed to call them. He said he fucked up seven cops before being placed successfully under arrest, and as he said this last part, he looked around

46

at everyone to see if anyone had spotted his lies. He woulda kept on, but one guy interrupted him.

"Man, stop bullshittin', Seven. Ya little ass, man one police banged ya eye," and everyone laughed in unison at this, "ripped ya shirt, stop bullshitting."

Leroy apparently didn't like being the butt of this joke, and without warning, he reached over and slapped the chubby guy's face twice and the rumble ensued. The Chubby guy got up, charged Leroy with the force of a bull, and they stood there, locked together and trying to free themselves while everyone else crowded around, saying, "Shhh, we don't want the guards to come."

The chubby guy freed himself and returned the two blows he had received from Leroy. Then they lost their balance and fell on the filthy concrete floor. The fight became boring after it was determined a wrestling match instead of the swift boxing match it had appeared to be at its start. The other guys peeled them apart, and both assailants looked pretty much unscathed as they stood opposite each other, still breathing uncontrollably.

"Only reason I didn't bag ya fat ass is 'cause I didn't wanna leave a mark!" Leroy screamed in between pants. This drew a scattered chuckle around the cell. The chubby dude, whose name was actually Chubby Jones, sat quietly peeling his orange as if nothing had happened. Only thing linking him to the skirmish was his slightly wrinkled T-shirt and his heavy breathing.

"Man, fuck you, liar," he said minutes later, as if an afterthought. This drew the same chuckle that Leroy had drawn. The couple guys who wanted to see round two would never get their wish.

After a long silence with only an occasional rustling of a bag or urine splashing into the toilet, another obese woman opened the door.

"One phone call a piece, three at a time," she sang out. This almost started another altercation as seven guys bumrushed the door. A little pushing and shoving ensued and four guys were herded back into the cell. I stayed behind; figuring the last set of three would get to make two quick calls.

I was right, and when it came time for the last set, Chubby, Leroy, and myself walked out, smirking at the others. An embracing handshake and hug was exchanged between Leroy and Chubby; the tension wore off now that they weren't in the cage anymore—at least for the time being.

I immediately called Toni, for these were not the collect call-only phones. Toni's grandmother had a collect call block. Toni's distraught voice answered on the third ring and it dawned on me that she wasn't at work.

"Toni, it's Donny," I said meekly to her. "What happened?" I tried to control my anger, but this bullshit was stressing me out.

"Baby, I'm so sorry. I paged you last night, like twenty times wit' my code, I called ya phone, I tried to tell ya that my grandmother was off work and she was going to be looking for my car. Why didn't you call me back, Cream?" I thought about rejecting her calls when I was with the hookers. Obviously, I couldn't tell her that.

"My battery in my phone was dead and I lost my pager fighting last night. Yeah, some niggas said I was lying about dating you so I slapped him two times." I went on, repeating everything I had just witnessed between Chubby and Leroy in the cell.

"Oh, baby, who was it?" Toni, concerned, wanted to know. Then she said, "Listen, I told her you had my car. I'm going to get her to drop the charges, and I'll bail you out if necessary, okay sweetheart? Are you hating me? Is everything still good between us?" she lamely asked.

"Just get me outta here," I told her. "Call the police station, tell them officer R. J. Sunto locked me up, explain, maybe they'll come get me out. What time is it?" I asked her.

"One-thirty," she replied and then went on. "Baby, my grandmother had my car, but I'm a come down there and pick you up when you get out, okay? I love you," she said and I hung up. I began berating myself for brushing her off for two dope fiend hookers. I had become cocky and it had kicked me right in my ass. I hurriedly called Steve next while the C.O. wasn't looking.

"Yo, Steam, it's me. You won't believe where I am. In the Bookings. Yo, I had Toni's car, got pulled over for speeding, and they searched the car and found the dope I was taking to Rock," I lied to him.

"Nigga, that's eighty grams; about thirteen thousand is gone. So you probably won't get a bail, huh?" Steve asked, frustrated.

"Hey, call the cleaners. Tell him I'll be late in getting the clothes," I changed the subject, but Steve wasn't havin' it.

"Man, you mean to tell me ya brother was gonna buy all that dope in one dip?" he challenged me.

"Yeah, I was gonna give him all of it for ten," I defended my lie, "but we'll work some shit out when. . . ." and then the phone was abruptly hung up by one of the cops. So caught up in my lies to Steve, I didn't notice I was the only one left in the hallway. Chubby and Leroy had been escorted back to the cell five minutes ago. She had been standing there, listening to me the whole time.

"Does 'jail' show up on caller ID?" I weirdly asked her, to try to hide my embarrassment at being caught.

"Yeah," she laughed. "Now get back in there," she said and slammed the door behind me. *Good. Steve will buy my story,* I thought.

Chapter 10

After twenty-five minutes of bargaining, the younger of the brothers, Harold, revealed the sought-after information. He admitted he did all the dealings for Sonny's operation and that Sonny paid them one thousand for ten days' worth of part-time work. He also said that Officers Dain and Sunto received a discount for their inside information on when there was going to be a raid or where there was surveillance. The guy posing as Chris was a friend named James, who wasn't on the customer list, and the brothers knew Chris was in New York and supposedly living there, so they lied to Sonny. He also said that Sonny and Landra occasionally used the dope themselves and that they were all partying on the night of the murders. Also, Sonny never told them about the arsenal of weapons he had stashed in the apartment. If anything, he downplayed what he had. The money in the safe was from last month's layout, and Sonny had sold a vehicle for fifteen thousand dollars.

"Sonny only makes fifty thousand dollars on his trips and takes the money every other month. Then he splits it, so it should've been sixty-five grand in that safe," Wollen pointed out.

Taylor gave Wollen a concerned look as she remembered the different amount that had been reported. Harold continued his story.

"We've been with Sonny for three years now, every month for his entire stay. He was selling pounds of weed for seven hundred dollars, and he brought forty-two with him; we sold every ounce, gram, and kilo for that man. He trusts his business with our judgment. Plus, he also gave out a gram of pure, uncut every night for us to split. That's why the pay was so low," he explained.

"We believe everything except the 'James' part. No body has been recovered, and we've kept a close tab on gunshot victims in the local hospitals. Tell me, what could you lose by staging a robbery?" Wollen confronted him with a bemused smile on his face.

"Our lives!" Harold blurted out.

"But you just said he had downplayed his arsenal of guns, which meant you felt it was low risk with high reward," Wollen suggested.

"We had only done eight thousand dollars in two days; it wouldn't be worth it," Harold objected.

"Sure it would. Ounces of raw dope can be stepped on three, four, and five times, and trash bags of weed? Shit. The safe money was a gamble, but you informed the stickup men about the dough. That's why they bought rope and tape to tie up Sonny and beat his girl until he told them the code!" Wollen shouted.

Suddenly, there was a loud knock at the door; Bunning had grown tired of waiting and wanted in on this interrogation. Taylor opened the door and invited him in. Harold's heat dropped at the sight of Bunning. The man obviously terrified the younger brother. Bunning walked quietly to an open chair, sat down, and waved his hands for them to continue. Wollen did.

"You only told the guys to bring one guy, 'cause you thought Sonny wasn't strapped like that. But Sonny was a smart man, smarter than you, right Harold?" Wollen jeered. He was so close to a confession, he could almost feel his penis become erect, but Harold was full of cheap dope and determined to lie until his grave.

"No, sir," he sniffed, obviously scared.

Taylor was very observant throughout all of this, watching the exchange, and she smelled a rat, yet she couldn't pinpoint from which hole he had run.

"Harold, we all know you are scared about the murders. You don't wanna go to jail for the rest of your life, do you?" Taylor asked.

"No," Harold, for once, answered honestly.

"Okay. Ms. Dixon killed herself, son. You're our only hope. We can be a team, instead of just you and your brother rotting in prison. Let the bastards who pulled the trigger do it. They got all the prize money and dope, right?"

"Yeah," he said, looking puzzled. She had tricked him and it had worked. She continued. "Okay, then. You got used, now you're about to do fifteen years to life in prison and you didn't even get a shake of the profit. You won't get your one thousand dollars and half gram of dope anymore. Haha. You got fucked and you haven't even gotten to prison yet."

"Yeah, you might wanna cut that long hair of yours," Bunning added sarcastically.

An unexpected noise was heard, and it was the door opening. It was Harold's dad, an older man with horn-rimmed glasses and a brown beret. He was slightly tan and a bit bulky, and he never returned the greeting he received from Harold's company. Instead he took a brown bag that had a plant in it and headed downstairs to the basement and shut the door. He had never said a word.

"He's weird," Harold admitted. "He and Mom haven't spoken in, like, two years. He lives in the basement."

"Harold, we should, and we probably will, lock you up. You'll be charged with obstruction of justice, for withholding vital information on a double homicide at the very least. But probably as an accessory, and maybe even the big M. But I have faith that you'll prevent that by coming forth with any more information, and I suggest you tell your brother the same thing," Taylor wrapped up.

As the three detectives got up to leave, Bunning turned back and said, "See you tomorrow at 8:00 on North Avenue, homeboy," he winked. Harold began wondering if his home was wired or his phones tapped. He shook his head, no, but still with caution as he watched the detectives from hell leave his house. Watching them board their Suburban through his Venetian blinds, Harold called for Ronnie.

"What?" he answered back.

"I'm scared, Ronnie. They're trying to take us down for that shit," Harold told his big brother.

"Man, fuck them. I'm getting high," Ronnie said and started back for the steps.

"Fuck it, I guess that makes two of us," Harold said as he joined his brother.

* * *

With many prayers and the passing of ten hours in Central Booking, I managed to convince the commissioner of my innocence and was granted bail on my own recognizance. Within an hour of this good news, I was returned my property and released. I began thanking God the police did not include the weed on my charge papers. My stylish clothing and schoolboy manners had won over the older white lady. A weed charge would have given a dark tint to my light of innocence.

I removed my cell phone from the manila envelope and called Toni's house. At the sound of her grandmother's voice, I restrained myself from cursing her out and just hung up. Now was definitely not the time to argue with that woman. It was a little after 7:00 P.M. by this time and I hoped my car was ready. I checked my voice mail. Yes! Mr. P. had left two messages and he had a ticket for the game; he even left his cell phone number. I hurriedly called the number he had left.

"Hello, Mr. P.," I said when he answered. "I'll be there in an hour. You have a ticket for me?"

"Ohhh, yeah I do. Give me an hour," he said. This was stupid, I thought, because the game had started at three o'clock.

"Okay, thanks," I said to him and hung up. I was so weak-minded and I tried to put it off and deny the obvious, but I needed a blunt. I needed a blunt to think clearly, sort of like a high school principal needed that morning cup of coffee before announcements. My mouth began to water at the thought of smoking a Dutch to the head.

Shit, I'm broke, I remembered. *I'll have to go home to get some more weed and money and to change my clothes.* I told my conscience that I was taking us out to Phillips Seafood in the Inner Harbor tonight. And I would stay at Harbor Court as a treat. My conscience accepted my date and I walked to the corner of Greenmount, where five hackers, having seen the manila folder and knowing I had just been released, signaled to me. No, thanks. With my luck today, a little old lady would rob me. I scanned the street for a legitimate cab and finally a Royal Cab caught my signal. I jumped in the bulletproof vehicle and directed him to GoodNow Road Apartments.

"Bad area," the driver told me. "Money up front."

"Look, hold my cell phone and wallet. I'm flat broke. I swear I will run in and get it and be right back out." He wasn't having it and kicked me back out on the corner.

"Please. Just two blocks north," I begged. The driver wasn't buying it though and he sped off, leaving me to question my extreme misfortune over the past thirty-six hours. *Fuck it, a hack will have to do,* I thought as I waved my hand like there was something stuck to it. An old man in a Buick pulled over. Upon entering his car, I noticed his dick hanging out between his zipper and his eyebrows wriggled at me.

"Oh no, motherfucker, let me out, now!" I demanded and he obliged.

"Take your faggot ass to Calvert Street," I yelled at him as he pulled off.

What the fuck? Do I look gay? I shoulda chopped that bitch off and made him eat it, but then I woulda had to touch it. As a Checker Cab sped past me, I wondered if I was going to make it home by noon tomorrow. Fuck this shit, I broke down and called Rock. I hated asking him for favors because he often made excuses to say no. But tonight I would plead my case with him and even offer up a six-pack of Heinekens and a quarter ounce of weed.

When he answered the phone, a woman could be heard in the background.

"Yo, I need you, I'm. . . ." I started off and then the phone went dead. What the fuck? I looked at the screen and noticed the low battery light flashing. I had to burst out laughing, if only to prevent me from crying softly to myself at my misfortune today. My mind was being stretched to elastic proportions and I began walking toward my apartment. It would take four hours on foot, at best, but I was determined to get home.

As I walked around, staring at the ground, I didn't notice the small crowd gathered adjacent from me, staring openly. My demeanor didn't fit the neighborhood, I guess, and neither did my clothes, and I stuck out like a cold sore on a pretty bitch.

"Yo, who dat?" I heard someone ask and I looked up to see four young kids dressed in clothes three sizes too big.

"Nobody," I told them and kept on walking.

"Well then, nobody need that sweater but me, so take it off!" Before he had ever finished this last line, I was running at full speed. No time for negotiating, I was not liking the turn their conversation had taken and wasn't in the mood to be rolled by four punks. The boys took off after me. Thanks to a little athletic prowess and just plain fear, I ran fast, but in my loafers with no socks and abused lungs, I began to slow down. I felt the boys closing in on me so I cut into this alley and decided to zigzag my way through and then just hide. To my surprise, luck finally came on my side. A police car rode by and spotted the foxes chasing their rabbit, and she flashed her lights and started after the pack of boys. They dispersed and then disappeared, but I made sure I stayed clearly visible. As she pulled up beside me, I heard chants of laughter and the hollering of cowardly names being directed at me. I held my manila envelope like football and thanked her for stopping. I explained what had happened and she advised me just to get outta the area.

"Listen, can you drive me three blocks, just to get outta this neighborhood?" I begged her. "I'll be fine from there."

"I'm not permitted to take riders, but I can radio you a cab," she offered.

"That's even better!" I thanked her and couldn't believe I was being so solicitous with the cops. I hated the cops.

Within minutes a tattered, broke-down-looking cab pulled up and a Pakistani named Mohammed jumped out and opened my door, like a chauffeur. I turned to thank the cop one more time, but she was already gone so I dove in the cab before the pants-hanging gang could return.

It was twenty minutes to eight and we drove peacefully. I had promised Porter an hour. We arrived at my apartment and he told me to take my time, that the meter would be running (of course!). I ran in, grabbed two hundred dollars, a "We R One" sweatsuit, some Timberland boots, and a handful of weed. I rushed back out and had Mohammed, the Pakistani cabbie, drive me to Essex. The total fare was sixty dollars, but I slid him a hundred-dollar bill, giving him a forty dollars tip for reasons he would never understand and I wasn't going to tell him.

It was 8:36 and Mr. P.'s lights were still on. Upon answering my knock at the door, I remembered the large amount of weed and pistol I had to transport. Dammit.

"Nephew, I was starting to close up shop," he told me, but I heard giggling which told me he wasn't about to close up his shop at all. "Your car been ready since morning, all that shit in the trunk still there. Here," he said and tossed me the keys. "Nothing personal, but pretend you never even met me. Tell Steve, Joey, and all them little fuckers that Mr. P. said bye-bye to all his little nephews. Oh, and here," he handed me two-hundred fifty dollars. Huh?

"Where's the rest?" He owed me more money; I might be unlucky, but I wasn't stupid.

"Son, I leave business at 6:00 P.M. sharp. I waited. That costs, you know," Mr. Porter gave me a convincing look. He had really used the two-hundred fifty dollars to pay for a beating with a bull whip and to receive anal pleasure by a dildo-wearing hooker; probably the one who was heard giggling.

"No, fuck that. Give me somethin' more. Enough is enough. I've had it with ya absurd rates on everything," I angrily told him. His greed was really starting to piss me off.

"Son, take this two hundred fifty and get out my shop before I cut your ass," he replied, unamused by my outburst. "I washed blood off ya hands, remember? Besides, look at your car, I deserve a tip," he told me.

"Man, fuck you," I stomped outta the lobby and jumped in my car, accelerating unnecessarily out of the garage. My car had a strong scent of cherries and the carpet and upholstery *was* sparkling. It reminded me of when I had bought the 1996 2.5 TL brand spanking new and I was happy again.

I successfully managed to transport the weed and the gun back to my apartment. I went in, only to grab clean underclothes and my toothbrush. I purposely left my cell phone, pager, and all of my worries behind. I rolled out and smoked the finest roll of marijuana I had ever had. I had been saving it for a special occasion.

As promised to myself, I arrived at Phillips Seafood at 9:40 and ordered the Crabcake Imperial, stuffed shrimp, and steamed lobster. I drank Hennessey and Coronas until I was green. The bill was eighty-five dollars and I left a hundred on the table and left.

The room would cost $189 and it was well worth it. Entering my suite, I figured I would top the night off with a wild night of sex. I called Toni.

"Toni," I said when she answered, "listen. Room 128, Harbour Court, bring ya ass over here now! Don't wear no drawers, no bra, and no socks. And hurry the fuck up, you hear me?" I said seductively into the phone.

"I'm on my way, Donny," she said and hung up. I sat back and lit a Dutch and clicked on the TV until an hour had passed. I heard the soft ring of the phone and picked it up.

"Guest for room 128, sir," the front desk told me.

"Send her up!" I told him, turning off the TV and light.

Chapter 11

I awoke to the phone ringing at eight thirty; the hotel service reminding me about the free breakfast buffet that started at nine. Toni was nowhere to be found. In her place lay a small piece of paper and on it was written at short note, expressing thanks for her "lovely and gorgeous" evening and an apology for having to go in to work. Evidently the large consumption of alcohol had produced an award-winning performance out of her body. I didn't recall the last time I made love for two hours before ejaculating, but when the time came, the liquor gave me courage to demand it in her mouth. My order was gladly accepted and filled, and the next thing I remember is passing out cold, drooling from the orgasm.

I had decided to face my fears instead of run from them, rationally deciding to make a trip to Delaware to holla at Steve and gamble. I desperately needed to begin selling the free weed for my rent, car payment, and insurance, and my time-share payment was due any day now. My extravagant lifestyle and my lucrative business pushed my monthly expense to well over three thousand.

I quickly dick and balled and dressed hurriedly, ready to start my day early and work late into the night. I declared today as "Hustlin' Day." I packed my small bag up and left out, purposely leaving Toni's nasty note for the housekeeper to read.

Breakfast was acceptable, nothing to get excited about—your typical scrambled eggs, bacon, and pancakes with an assortment of fresh fruit. I ate the silver dollar pancakes and the beef sausage slowly, trying to make every bite last as I contemplated my plans for the day. Too much pressure was straddling my shoulders and the lukewarm breakfast didn't help it. Last night had been good, I decided, but the misfortune of being arrested added to the reality of my dumb mishap rode me like Vanessa Del Rio.

Finally, I got up, left a tip, and headed out. I returned the key card and flashed the desk lady my famous smile.

"Sleep well, Mr. Wise?" she asked.

"Yes, ma'am, and the breakfast was delicious," I lied.

"I see you had company last night, to assist you in sleeping well, I presume?" she flirted.

"Well, I gave you the elevator eyes, but you passed me up. So you know. . . ." I trailed off, flirting back with her.

"Next time I'll be more attentive to your overtures, Mr. Wise," she said as she finished checking me out. I took the comment in stride and walked outside, where my car was waiting in the turnaround. The bellboy reached for my bag as soon as he saw me exiting, and I knew it was a ploy just to get a tip. I slid him five bucks and jumped in the car, pulling off to begin another day of risky business.

I entered my Cedonia apartment and robotically reached for a Dutch while reading the morning *Baltimore Sun*. I called Steve's dorm but didn't get an answer, so I flipped through the paper until I found the sports section. The Orioles lost again, so I was glad I did miss the game, I thought, stupidly forgetting that I never actually had a ticket in the first place. As I started crafting my Dutch, I read over an article about the Ravens. How we had a historic defense and the article made mention of a free agent quarterback who was signed to improve our mediocre offense. I sparked the Dutch and coughed; the weed was beginning to make my twenty-one-year-old body feel old. I walked into my little efficiency kitchen and opened a half gallon of OJ, daydreaming about which bird I would become. Would I be another Baltimore Raven, underdogged but designed for success? Or would I be an Oriole, tattered with the potential of success but succumbing to meager results by underachieving and giving up? I continued to ponder this as I dragged on the Dutch between sips of OJ.

The phone rang; it was Fats and I jumped at the opportunity to unload some of this weed. After arranging to meet Fats at the closest KFC, I went for the stolen, free weed stash and then stopped. He'll notice it's Sonny's weed and link me. So I redirected my steps and grabbed a pound of my own weed. I decided to walk to KFC to break in my new pair of 'buttas" I was wearing.

Fats was waiting there patiently, although I was twenty minutes late.

"Hear any more 'bout them killings?" I asked him as I approached.

"Naw, I think this girl set him up," he responded, uninterested.

"Okay, I gotta hurry. I'm busy," I rushed him. I was too big for Fats's company now and he knew it. After becoming very wealthy from a lead poisoning suit, Fats had become too arrogant and uncouth. He dressed vaguely, developed an Ecstasy habit, and chose to live in his parents' home while selling his weed, which I personally found very trifling and lame. Rumor was he lost twenty thousand dollars in Vegas, trying to play Big Shot at the blackjack tables, and that the loss had broke him.

I strolled back to my apartment the long way, enjoying the budding trees and sunshine. *Please help me feel better about myself,* I begged the sun.

Once again I had forgotten to take my phone with me to meet Fats, and it was ringing furiously when I entered the apartment. It was probably just a chick who wanted me to come and get her, so I let the machine pick it up. I was right. After she had hung up, I called Steve again and his roommate answered.

"Put Grovehand on the phone," I demanded, referring to Steve's last name.

"Okay," he answered. "Hey, Groovey! Phone! I think it's Pistol," the roommate guessed wildly.

"Hey, what up, Pistol?" Steve laughed as he came on the phone.

"Tell that wild ass coon don't assume shit," I couldn't help it, but I laughed with him.

"Man, we need to talk, Creamy. The jakes are putting heat on my boys," he told me.

"What boys?" I asked. What boys was he talking about?

"All right," he sighed. "Remember when I told you about the heist? And Chris? And what all was in there?" he asked me.

"Yeah, but you never told me who put you on," I responded. I didn't like the turn this convo was taking either.

"Well, anyways, it was a good friend of mine."

"Who?" I demanded.

"Ronnie Finx," he answered.

"And?" I prompted him.

"Well, he told me to say Chris because the real Chris had moved to New York. But the cops found him and are now pressuring Ronnie and his brother, Harold," he confessed.

"There's two of 'em?" I practically screamed.

"Yeah, little brother Harold is just a tagalong, though. Anyway, their cut was supposed to be half of the dope we got and a thousand dollars. They said we could keep all the weed."

"Why did you only say it was a coupla pounds and a few thousand?" I asked him.

"Because I didn't want Pistol to know. I was only going to give him five hundred dollars, no matter what we scored," he answered honestly.

I laughed, "I shoulda known that."

"So the dope's gone and it was supposedly some strong shit from Florida, taking a four or even a five, so they want their dope now and you say it's gone," Steve informed me. "I'm afraid they may suspect a pullover and go state," he concluded.

"Just give them some money," I instructed Steve.

"Well, he said not to come around there 'cause of the cops. He made me promise to save their dope. I didn't tell you because I wanted them to remain behind the scenes, but with Pistol getting killed and all, it fucked everything up. Pistol was supposed to be my stash house," Steve complained. "Ronnie called from the payphone on North Avenue, saying the cops had wired his home phone."

"How he know?" I asked.

"'Cause they heard him telling his girl to go get dope at eight o'clock in the morning and the cops mentioned it to him later that day." He took a long pause and I could hear him mutter, "What the fuck?" He was smoking too. "You fucked us up, nigga," he said.

His paranoia was pissing me off and so were his accusations, like it was my fault the heist got blown all to shit. I wanted to cut him off and hang up on him, but eventually, my heat died down enough and I was able to say, "Yo, if I woulda had my car, the police wouldn't have found the dope. Toni's grandmother reported the car stolen and I unknowingly drove the car around and got pulled over for speeding," I lied angrily to him. The thought of my best friend holding out on me with vital information was infuriating me. I was getting madder by the second. "And," I went on, outraged, "*tell them fuckin' dope fiend junkies to look out for shotguns next time they want some free blow! Fuck them blow-sniffin' bitches and fuck you too!*" I screamed into the phone. I wanted to slam it down to further express my anger, but it was a cell phone and I had to be content with punching the "End" button as hard as I could and throwing it on the bed.

It immediately rang again and I was ready to accept any challenge that Steve could threaten me with. Instead, he was apologetic when I answered with a loud, rude, "What?"

"I'm sorry, yo, you're right. They could've gotten us killed. All they thought about was a free forty grams of raw, but we can't say 'fuck em,' Cream. They're white, we're black, they'll run to the cops quicker than Carl Lewis," he told me.

"We? You, nigga!" I corrected him.

"We'll just have to give them a coupla thousand more," Steve said.

"Well, look, I have five grand for you right now, not including the weed," I told him.

"Give them whatever you want; let's split up this weed and you can have the gun. Yours is melted," Steve offered.

"Great. No, I don't want it. For sure. You keep the gun."

"I can't believe we only got eight thousand. He said twenty thousand," Steve whined some more about the failed heist. I flash backed to the scene and remembered I was the one who had taken the one thousand dollars Pistol was fronted to make the fake buy. I ran to the hamper and grabbed the Girbaud jeans I had been wearing that night, and sure enough, there in my back pocket, perfectly creased, were ten hundred-dollar bills. I miraculously calmed down and began reminiscing about that night. It had totally dominated my thinking and I had forgotten I had stashed a G in my pocket during all the commotion.

"I don't wanna go near either one of them; the cops are probably watching every move they make. I'll get a girl to call and tell them to meet us at Clemmy's Saturday night. The cops won't be in there and we can map some numbers," Steve said.

"Tomorrow night, I am going on vacation. I'll stay to give you your five grand and divide the smoke and then I'm out," I bluntly told him.

"Where you goin'?" Steve asked. "I'll go with you," he offered.

"North Carolina," I lied as I pictured Atlanta, Georgia, in my mind. "I'm going to see my dad," I lied further to block out any more potential self-invites. "Aight yo, I got some business, so. . . ." I trailed off.

"Aight, you still heated, man?" he asked before I could hang up the phone.

"Naw, Mo, we cool." I said what he wanted to hear so I could get off the phone. *I never woulda thought, man . . .* as I pictured Steve threatening to shoot the guys, the white girl screaming in terror, Sonny's and Pistol's blood smeared all over the walls. "All for this shit," I said looking at the trash bags full of plants. Before sorrow could overcome me again, I jumped up and grabbed a baseball hat and my car keys. I had business to do and drugs to sell. *My life is miserable*, I thought to myself as I removed the large amount of cash from the transaction with Fats to put in my safe. I checked my pager and saw that there were a few from the old man, one from Mink, and some from a coupla other people.

I weighed out the final two pounds of the weed I had gotten honestly and two pounds of the ill-gotten weed that had caused so much bloodshed. I picked up the phone and called my good friend Braino, an avid gun collector, and proposed the deal of a lifetime. A .45 and an ounce of weed for a Davis .380 and two clips loaded with anything but hollow-tips.

"It has a body, I presume?" Braino asked after I had explained the deal I wanted.

"No," I defended, "it's just the owner of one." I giggled but he still didn't catch on.

"Okay, deal. Come over," he told me.

"Great, I'm on my way. I'll even throw in two boxes of hollow-tips." I promised him as I hung up. I grabbed the contraband and stuffed it all into my backpack.

As I was hutting the door to my apartment, I decided that this was the day for some hard hustlin' but not the day to go down for a murder. I decided that after I had sold every gram, I would go to Fells Point and drink myself into a stupor.

Chapter 12

There I was, drunk as hell, sitting in the living room of some white girl's house. I think her name was Christina, but I wasn't sure. I would find out shortly, It had been twenty-four hours of constant running around, selling weed. Exactly eight pounds, a pint of Belvedere French vodka, and seven thousand dollars later, I met Christina at a bar in Fells Point. She was rolling off E and I was drunk off Belvee, and somehow we managed to make it back to her house to do the nasty.

"You're finally awake, sleepy head," a soft voice said from the direction of the kitchen. A cloud of cigarette smoke had led me to her. She was short redhead, and her obesity wouldn't have met my standards under normal and sober conditions. Alcohol has a way of making one over look someone's physical misfortunes.

My head began pounding as I looked at my watch: 8:58.

"You hungry, sweetheart?" Christina, I think, asked me.

"Yeah, fix me a Dutch Master Deluxe, hold the Mayo," I joked, and she laughed loudly as she peeked out at me. With the exception of my ankle socks and my designer Joe Boxers, I was naked. My penis hung limply though the opening of my boxers. She brought out a BLT with a large glass of orange juice for me and placed the tray on the coffee table as I started toward the food.

"You want it now, or after you eat?" she asked me.

"What?" I asked, puzzled.

"What you told me last night."

"What was that?" I asked her, still having no clue what she was talking about.

"You told me last night while we were fuckin' that you wanted your dick sucked during breakfast, 'member?"

"Oh yeah. Yeah, I want it now," I told her as I positioned myself so I could eat and be blessed at the same time. She dropped down to one knee and took my penis into her mouth. Usually a fast eater, you can see why I decided to take my sweet time during this breakfast. This fat chick's a pro, I fantasized, keeping my eyes opened while sipping the orange juice, which I almost spilled. I felt a sensation run through my leg and I began moaning loudly, a signal of what was soon to come. The semen shot out like a cannon, and like an experienced package handler, Christina kept doing her job. The reality of just coming in her mouth overwhelmed me and I began to shake uncontrollably, having an orgasm. She continued her services and began to moan like a wounded cat. The continuation of her sucking and her moaning sent a tingle throughout my whole body and my eyes rolled back as I felt myself about to come. Again.

"I'm about to come," I whispered to her, slobbering because I just couldn't help myself. This time, she withdrew my penis from her mouth and come began shooting everywhere, hitting her in the face. She rubbed it all over her face, smearing it everywhere and all over her lips and mouth. I fell out of the chair at this sight, landing flat on my back and into a deep euphoria as I watched this chick do something I had never seen before.

* * *

Detective Taylor, Captain Tim Sanders, and Chief Stewart Lincoln sat in a conference room, patiently awaiting the arrival of Officer R.J. Sunto. Officers Dain and Porton were schedule to meet with them at 11:00 and 12:00.

Sunto entered, his uniform pressed and cleaned and his boots shined because he thought he was here for a promotion.

Detective Taylor started off the meeting with explaining everything that was found inside Sonny's rented Cadillac. As Sunto became uneasy about the turn this meeting was taking, Taylor slid Sonny's customer list at him. He began to sweat from his brow and started to hyperventilate. He felt like he could not get enough oxygen. After Taylor's presentation, the African-American captain began explaining the department's policy on corrupt cops and the policies on officers and drug use.

"But this list is not sufficient evidence!" Sunto stuttered, interrupting the captain. Taylor slid another piece of paper to him.

Sunto stared dumbfounded at the paper, knowing everything in it was true. The captain resumed his lecture and the department's intolerance of illegal activities by their officers.

"I am recommending you for immediate termination and revocation of your pension," the captain told a crushed Sunto.

Sunto stared at the chief with a repentant and remorseful look upon his face. His eyes begged the chief to overlook the recommendation. The older white man, who resembled Leslie Nielsen with a mustache, just returned the pitiful look with stone cold eyes. He was not to be swayed.

The captain kept on, going into the integrity of the entire department and how trust and honesty were never to be regained after something like this. Then he paused and looked to the chief, who nodded his head slowly.

"Recommendation granted. Termination is to be enforced immediately. Give me your badge and gun. Now," the captain told Sunto as he was handed a plastic bag to put his belongings in. Taylor discreetly removed her pistol, just in case Sunto decided to go postal on everyone. Sunto cried tears of shame as he handed over his beloved badge and his police issued 9 mm Glock. His tears were his confession.

"The hearing for your pension termination will be held ten days from today. You will be notified by the Board when and where to appear. You were a good officer, Mr. Sunto, but all your pending arrests will be dropped or not processed because your integrity has been questioned. You are very lucky, because we could bring criminal charges against you," the Captain gravely said as there was a loud knock at the door and Wollen entered.

"Wollen, please take Mr. Sunto to his locker, help him clean it all out, and see him to the door," Taylor instructed Wollen, who was happy he was selected for this duty. "Have a nice life, dirtbag," Taylor told him scornfully.

It was exactly 10:58.

"One down, two to go." Captain Sanders remarked sadly. To avoid notice, Sunto was escorted left and Dain was directed to come from the right.

After two hours of animated crying, pleas, and flat out begging, the Baltimore Police Department had lost three of its officers.

Porton, unaware of Sunto and Dain's termination and the evidence held by the brass, had tried to offer information about their drug use, even volunteering to wear a body wire to record a conversation. She stopped cold when the captain coldly told her, "That won't be necessary, Ms. Porton. You are terminated as well, and I am recommending that your pension be revoked."

As she was exiting the conference room, she faked a blackout and crumpled to the floor. Wollen, suppressing a smile, bent to help her up, seeing her eyes flutter as she tried hard to remain "unconscious." Finally she gave it up and got back to her feet. Since Wollen was not permitted in the women's locker room, Taylor would have to carry out this duty and she got to her feet. Wollen, expecting another show, followed closely behind, laughing silently to himself at the lengths to which some people would go.

Porton made one last stand while she was being escorted out the door. "I only smoke because of my glaucoma. Don't fire me—I have four children at home," the plump, dark-skinned woman begged. She was finally dragged to her car, where she relented long enough to scream "Fuck all ya'll" and speed off while a small crowd had gathered to watch.

Taylor and Wollen laughed until their eyes teared and their stomachs ached. The scene had been hilarious. Detective Bunning paged Taylor; he was curious about the outcome of the meetings with the corrupt cops. Wollen got out his small phone and flipped it open and called Bunning back. He was still laughing about the scene and Bunning answered to a wild array of laughter.

"Well, Wollen, what happened?" he anxiously inquired.

After a few more whimpers of laughter, Wollen chokingly explained Ms. Porton and her eventful departure. Bunning failed to see the humor in it, really.

"I guess you had to be here," Wollen said, gaining his composure. "What's up?" he asked Bunning.

"The brothers got a call from some chick telling them to meet tonight at a night club out on Charles Street. The older brother talked quickly and before he hung up, he muttered, 'They better have my shit.' We'll be there, follow the brothers home, and have a patrol car pull them over and hope and pray we recover some of the dope from the murders."

"Sounds good to me," Wollen answered and Taylor agreed; she had been listening on speakerphone. "Meet us at Star's for coffee in an hour so we can put our thoughts together and come up with a game plan."

"Cool," Bunning said and he hung up.

* * *

I woke up to my pager buzzing loudly. It was 1:45 P.M. and Christina was sleeping peacefully next to me. I tiptoed to my belongings and dressed quickly, trying not to wake her. Steve had been paging me for an hour, and the thought of unloading the ill-gotten weed excited me. I made sure I had everything, for this was the last time Miss Piggy would see my yellow face. I did write her a quick thank-you note and told her to keep in touch (yeah right, like I had given her my numbers) and vanished out the back door, fearing the front door would awaken her as she slept in the living room. My car was parked strangely and I realized I hadn't driven to this place last night. I'm an excellent parker and I knew I never would have parked like this. I dialed Steve's number while driving down the block.

"Hey, Wody," I said to him when he picked up.

"Where the hell you been?" he demanded to know.

"Doin' the cha-cha with the white Nell Carter. Don't ask," I told him. He did anyway. "I got drunk down in Fells Point last night and met some bitch rolling off E. She kidnapped me, drove me to her house, and fucked and sucked me on command." I hesitated before telling him about breakfast, but I did anyway.

"Man, put me on. She a freak," Steve said.

"Okay, but let's meet up first. I'll go home, shower up, and come holla," I promised him.

"Okay, I'll be waiting."

My head was pounding as I pulled up to my apartment building; I was still a little hung over. I took a Motrin, rolled a small Dutch, and took a hot shower, scrubbing my body violently as I remembered Big Momma. I felt a lot better after taking the pill and my high set in.

Hmm, I feel like Kenneth Cole today, I thought as I examined my shoes. I threw on a traditional white Kenneth Cole T-shirt, baggy Kenneth Cole jeans, and rugged Rockport boots. I finished my outfit with my signature fitted Orioles cap.

After removing ten pounds of weed and Steve's five grand from my safe and stuffing them into my bookbag (dammit, it was hard for it all to fit!) I noticed that I had gotten some mail. A letter from the State of Maryland. Enclosed was a two-line paragraph, explaining that my charge had not been processed. The letter was signed by the prosecutor and dated yesterday.

"Thanks!" I yelled, practicing my hook shot with the balled up letter.

I rolled out, happy about the great news from the prosecutor, the splendid events of my morning breakfast, and ridding myself of this weed. Before hitting the highway, I stopped for some gas and a chicken box. Toni called my phone, angry at my disappearance after Thursday morning.

"Nigga, it's Saturday. Who you been wit'?" she demanded to know, but I cut her off.

"Shut up with that other bitch shit. Guess what! They're dropping the charges!" I gleefully told her to change the subject. "Hey, you wanna go to Clemmy's tonight?" I asked her.

"No."

"Good. Me neither. I'll pick you up and take you to the mall, okay?"

"Okay," she relented like I knew she would.

"Good, I'll call you later on today," I promised her, ripping into a chicken wing dripping with hot sauce. I hung up and resumed my trip, blasting Jay-Z on the radio.

I thought about my supposed trip to Atlanta. Fuck it, I'll leave tomorrow morning, I told myself, just me and Toni. I relaxed; the idea of a vacation made me smile. I loved to travel, especially on the spur of the moment like this. Just jumping up, grabbing money, clothes, and lots of weed, and just hitting the road. I would jump at the chance tomorrow.

"Peachtree Boulevard, here I come!" I promised.

Chapter 13

After picking up Steve and taking him to some girl's house to stash the weed, we headed toward White Marsh Avenue for a movie and some brunch at Friday's. Steve sparked up a cannon and, like his usual self, smoked on it by himself until I threatened to break his limbs. He finally passed it to me and I took a long drag and blew it in his face.

"Call the fellas from East Rock; tell them meet us at the mall," I told him.

He obliged and called Braino, Black, my brother Rock, and then Matt, one right after the other, They all agreed to meet us in front of the food court in an hour. After transforming from a company to a crowd, we rushed the theater because the movie was starting in ten minutes. Like true niggas, Black and Rock had sneaked two pints of Hennessey into the theater to enhance our mood a little, since smoking was obviously out.

The movie was funny, but the intoxication was better, I thought as I found myself drifting off into space. After a long doze, I was shoved on the shoulder.

"Get up, nigga, the movie over," Braino shoved me again. We all trailed out of the theater, staggering and laughing, recalling points in the flick, which I could not remember.

"I'm starvin'," Matt told us.

"Yeah, I know. Me too. Let's eat at Friday's," Steve suggested, even though that was our original plan.

We entered the well-known restaurant and were seated right away. Braino, the richest member of our entourage, volunteered to pay for everyone's drinks, including the table of three sexy ladies next to our booth. I wanted to pass on a drink but felt pressured, so I ordered a martini and a strawberry daiquiri. The ladies smiled when the waitress told them of Braino's considerate offer. Braino raised his hand a little and nodded to let the women know who their benefactor was.

We drank, ate, and then drank some more until our total bill was well over two hundred dollars. Matt, the wealthy Italian in our crew, gestured to the table of ladies that he would cover their entire tab, so as not to be outdone by Braino. The women, so intrigued by their outright generosity, came over to sit at our table, dragging chairs over.

The light-skinned bomb held the check in her perfectly manicured hand, and Matt gently took it from her and asked for her number. She wanted to say no, but the platinum watch and bracelet made her change her mind. The brown-skinned chick whispered "Thank you," into Braino's ear, which caused him to smile. His chain, crusted with baguettes, gleamed perfectly against his chest.

After an exchange of top-secret talk, Braino excused himself from the table and took the beautiful female by the hand and led her to the front of the restaurant. They could be seen walking to his car. Rock, being the original playa, pressed hard for the third chick. After a brief conversation on his cell phone and a quick check of his two-way pager, he turned his attention on her. The girl was so fat in her ass that she walked with a limp. Her face was dark, but her hair was beautiful, evidence that she had some Indian in her. Rock is known to possess the gift to gab, and he spoke to her quickly and expertly until Tonto displayed a perfect set of white teeth in a huge smile. She began digging through her leather bag while checking out the amount of empty glasses and plates on our table. *These niggas is ballers*, she thought to herself as she eagerly searched for the pen that had written hundreds of numbers.

Rock continued complimenting her while she wrote down her numbers.

"You better call me," her lovely voice sang out when she finished jotting down her information.

Rock, being the infinite player, handed her a business card. "That's my cell, two-way, and office phone right there. You better call me! Ma," he retorted as he winked at her. The only business Rock was involved in was selling dope, but the card presented a good front and it impressed the ladies.

After fifteen minutes of casual conversation, and waiting for their girlfriend to return, the women exchanged goodbyes with all of us and left. Finally Braino came sliding in past the ladies, waving goodbye to them.

"Yo, guess what! You won't believe this shit. Shorty starting suckin' my dick in the car!" Braino bragged.

"What?" we all said at once.

"Yeah, I wrote down my number for her and BOOM! She said she loved getting nasty in the Mercedes Benz and then she did her thing."

We all laughed at this and as usual, Steve sang out, "Yo, put me on, man."

Matt removed his large bankroll and flipped off six fifties, the two checks totaled $265 and the change was for the waitress's well-deserved tip. Like true businessmen, Rock and Black had immediate sales lined up and had to break from our afternoon of fun.

Matt and Braino agreed that it was time to get back to business and everyone exchanged hugs and handshakes.

"Yo, let's hook up tonight at the Wharf, my treat," Black bluffed.

"Yeah, I heard that one before," Rock said laughing. He and Black were close, and an offer like that from Black was not to be taken seriously. We continued to laugh at this as we made our way to our cars, which had turned the parking lot of this suburban Friday's into a celebrity driveway. Braino's big Benz S-420, Matt's pearl white Lexus GS-400, Rock's tricked-out champagne-colored Expedition with 20s and TVs, and Black's Jeep Grand Cherokee with its GPS and ski racks were parked next to my Acrua TL. Like all men, we all respected each other but still wanted to outdo each other, a natural trait among ballers.

* * *

Harold had started calling all the customers he had brought to Sonny in anticipation of the dope he was to receive.

"Yo, the Florida Gold is still in town, but it's going for one hundred fifty dollars a gram now. You better get back with me before the shit is gone," he told them all and the customers agreed on the stiff price, only because the shit was the best in the city. Harold and Ronnie had planned to chop off Sonny since day one, but Sonny's intimidating personality and his blatant threats to kill their family if they ever crossed him scared them. Sonny was the worst drug dealer ever to work for because he was greedy, but he also expected loyalty unto death. Every time the brothers would attempt to break from Sonny, the good heroin would be shoved in their faces and it would draw them back in. Sonny would only soften a little after he reached his fifty grand quota and would try to reassure them.

"Man, I don't have no guns, I would never hurt your mom and dad. I just be trippin' sometimes," he would laugh and then toss them a bag of dope and some more money. Then he and Landra would disappear again for weeks, only to return with a shitload of dope and the same greedy, evil attitude. His tyrannical rage was inflicted upon everyone except Landra, who knew what to say to calm him down.

Now, he was gone and Harold felt a burden of fear leave his chest when Sonny was gunned down. He just wished his stupid brother wouldn't have told the police so much. He firmly believed they would eventually be arrested, but the thought of free, raw dope made the risk worth all the trouble that was sure to follow.

After rounding up fifteen hundred dollars in sales, he sat back, thinking of what he was going to wear tonight. He hated black clubs; they made him feel weak and paranoid, but the idea of the dope gave him the strength to fight any black man alive.

Ronnie came through the door with Jenny. She had been too scared to tell him about the big black man who called himself Todd who had taken them to get their morning gate shot. She copped eight pills and had ingested one of them on the way home. She wondered why the black stranger didn't buy any dope for himself. Even more strange was why he didn't ask to do any of hers. He just wanted to ask questions about her boyfriend Ronnie. She regretted telling him so much about the package the brothers were supposed to receive tonight.

"Sonny's dope?" the stranger asked.

"Hell, yeah, I hope it's Sonny's dope. I don't know for sure though because Ronnie likes to beat me up when I ask about this business so I just leave it alone. He never tells me anything anymore," Jenny pouted.

I wonder why, Bunning, the black stranger thought.

"Hey, bro, what we got?" Ronnie asked Harold as he entered. Harold told him about the sales lined up. He handed Harold two pills and then yelled to Jenny, "Bitch, get upstairs when we talk, you too fuckin' nosy!" This woke her up out of her nod and she looked up and nodded and then walked quickly up the stairs. As soon as she was out of earshot, he whispered, "Did Steve call yet?"

"Nope," Harold answered as he sniffed the capsule of this morning's cheap dope. "This shit is garbage, Ron!" he complained.

"I know, but it will knock the monkey for awhile. Plus, tonight we'll have the good shit," Ronnie promised. Harold sniffed the remaining capsule.

"Yeah, I can't wait!" he agreed. The scrambled dope had hit Harold lightly and he felt himself nodding off. Ronnie, who had met Jenny at her house after she had claimed she had driven down to get some dope, nodded off peacefully as well.

"Hey, hey! Why the fuck did Sonny get those fuckin' guns?" Harold called out, weirdly. "The bastard lied to us! I never would have told Steve and Pistol to hit the house if I'd known Sonny had shot guns and shit back there," he whined.

"Yeah, we just woulda told him to bring a Tec-9," Ronnie laughed. The plan had seemed perfect. "Take the money, dope, and weed, tie us up, and leave. Sonny would have suspected Chris and would have paid us our money. He would've went back down to Florida with his safe money and his white bitch and come back, hunting for Chris, who would be safely in New York by that time. Eventually, he would've given up on finding Chris for only eight grand and a few ounces, and after a few idle threats, everything would be back to normal. But noooooo. The shit had to turn into fuckin' Camelot and shit," Ronnie whined some more about the ill-fated heist.

"Who was that guy? I told Steve only two people," Harold asked, remembering the Jamaican with the dreads.

"He wasn't Jamaican, dumbass; it was one of those fake dreadlock wigs," Ronnie scolded him.

"He did have a thick mustache though, didn't he?" Harold asked. "Anyway, I am glad he came; someone had to round up the money while Steve tied us all up. Pistol sure couldn't have." This drew a round of cruel laughter as Ronnie got up off the couch.

"I'm goin' to fuck, bro. Catch ya later," he said and went upstairs.

* * *

Thankfully, Steve was finished shopping. He had spent well over a thousand dollars of the five I had just given him. Clothes, tennis shoes and boots, and spring jackets cluttered my trunk. His continuous spree had spurred me to buy a pair of Air Max and a Skip Wise jersey before remembering my supposed trip in the morning.

We pulled off and Steve lit another cannon of a Dutch. This time he passed it to me without me giving him shit.

"How much you gonna give them dope fiends?" I asked him.

"Ummmm . . . fifteen hundred dollars a piece and I'll promise to find them some good blow after I sell some of this weed. I hope they don't buck," Steve said.

"They won't. What they gonna do? Call the police? They'll be the ones locked up, not us," I reasoned.

"So they'll take the money and then ride my ass until I find them some good dope," Steve prayed.

"I hope," I told him as I pulled on the huge blunt. Steve inserted the new Cash Money Millionaires CD he had just bought and sat back. The bass thumped the trunk and we couldn't help but bop to the Southern lyrics. The Dutch burned slow and the music jammed. I was beginning to feel better about myself.

"I'm going to be so fresh and clean in the spot tonight, my neezy," Steve bragged over the loud music.

"Bet. I'm not going," I sneaked that in as quick as I could, hoping he wouldn't notice. He did.

"What? Come on. You have to," he told me.

"I'm hookin' up with Toni tonight. I promised her."

"No, man, I need a ride to the hook-up with the brothers. Please?" he begged.

"I'll drop you off. Me and Toni," I offered.

"That freak?"

"Yeah," I defended. "I don't know, I might come in for a minute or two," I told him to appease him a little, but I knew that going to the club was completely against everything I wanted to do.

Chapter 14

After dropping Steve and the weed off, I called Toni to check the status of her readiness. She sounded delighted to hear my voice, calling me "baby" more than necessary. I sped through traffic, listening to the Hot Boys CD Steve had left in the car. The idea of Steve making me do yet another risky activity infuriated me, but since I was responsible for losing the dope in the first place, I felt obligated to go meet the brothers with him. The element of surprise might be too much for the brothers to handle, especially since we were talking about high-grade heroin here.

My earlier intoxication began to wear off and my mind became clear as I pictured Toni's beautiful body. I had slowly fallen in love with her throughout all this. The rumors of her freakiness I attributed to a young mind looking for attention, and besides, nobody I ran with had had her, so maybe the rumor was just that: a rumor. I drove to the beat, bobbing my head with the music, and a slight feeling of anxiety crept into me as I started thinking about those dope fiend brothers and our situation tonight. I wanted out so bad, yet I had allowed myself to sink too deep just to turn my back. My livelihood and freedom were at stake. *Why oh why did I do this dumbass caper?* My conscience screamed at me relentlessly. Sorrow filled me as I replayed the mind-boggling events of the failed heist, the sight and smell of Pistol's dead body, and the hookers clipping the dope.

I turned the music off and drove in silence. I thought about myself needing a change of direction; I thought about death, poisoned by the lure of fast money. Would it overtake me? Would I be another Sonny, killed for my drugs and money? I thought about my lost soldiers who were all gunned down senselessly, shot to death over illegal money. How did they view me from heaven? Was I just as bad as the persons who killed them? Was my passage to heaven denied because of my actions? I closed my eyes and asked God to forgive me. Before I knew it, I was pulling up at Toni's; the sight of her car made me angry again. I laid on the horn and Toni came out, looking gorgeous. It was obvious that she had been waiting by the window for me to pull up.

Toni was the type of woman who made me wanna change. She was so beautiful. I couldn't help the erection I got just staring at her. She had a college degree, a good paying job, and her wanton personality had moved me. She was always laughing at my dumb jokes, asking for piggyback rides across the street, revealing her perfect set of teeth before making love; everything about her became an emphasis. Her opening of the car door broke my trance and her repetitious and soft kisses further hardened my erection.

"Hey, sweet pea. What's wrong, baby?" she asked, concerned.

"You. I think I'm fallin' in love with you," I honestly told her.

"Oh, baby, I love you too," she replied, kissing both my cheeks warmly. I shifted into drive four and pulled off, heading toward the mall.

"You in the mood for some fun shopping tonight?" I asked her, unenthused. My earlier thoughts on the caper and what was to happen tonight had destroyed my jubilant mood beyond repair.

"You know I'm always ready for some shopping. What mall are we going to, baby?"

"I was thinking Owings Mills. They have the best stores, in my opinion."

"Yeah, you're right, honey," she agreed with me. To hide my depressed mood, I turned up the music to avoid conversation. I began waving my head to the beat. Toni, as always, laughed silently while examining my every move, her infatuation obvious.

The front worked. We didn't resume talking until I was pulling into a parking space at the mall. I had never spent money on a female before, for I always guarded myself against being used. But I felt very generous toward Toni, so I decided to spend around two hundred fifty dollars. I was old school, taught the more money you make, the less you spend on a female, for their natural attraction was more apparent. They only wanted money and we only wanted free pussy, so it's a cat and mouse game to determine the winner. That's why the ugliest men had the prettiest women. I wanted to sit in the car and smoke a blunt while Toni shopped freely, but I knew that wasn't an option. I had this problem with straying off in the mall, checking out the bad bitches who walked by. But Toni didn't deserve the dog treatment, not yet anyway.

We went from clothing stores to shoe stores to perfume counters. We went to fragrant candle shops and Toni shopped very conservatively, picking out stuff on sale whenever possible. I decided to give her the two hundred fifty dollars right off the top to avoid any embarrassment on her part. A dollar over two hundred fifty dollars would've been denied. *Shit, she lucky she getting this much*, I thought to myself as I pulled out the money.

After two hours of price checking and bargaining, Toni was finished. Thank God the mall was closing; she was acting like she had just gotten started. My arms and legs ached as I carried the five stuffed bags of shit she had purchased. She rubbed up against my ass gently when I popped the trunk to store her hefty baggage.

"You got a treat for Daddy tonight or what?" I asked her.

She smiled and rubbed my groin. "No." My penis was growing harder and harder with each of her touches.

"Please, please," I begged her as I flung open the car doors. Before we had even pulled off, she had loosened my belt buckle. I did my best to assist her struggle in getting my pants down, smiling down at her. We entered the flow of traffic on the highway and I reclined my seat slowly. Toni went to work.

"Yes, yes!" I danced happily and raised my groin into her mouth gently to show my ultimate appreciation. I wished I could have closed my eyes and enjoyed my pleasure, but driving seventy miles per hour blindfolded is not recommended if you want to live.

Toni peeked up and said, "Just tell me when we get to my street," and the thought of a nonstop twenty-minute blowjob aroused me to full strength.

"I hope I last that long," I told her, sounding more feminine than I preferred. She laughed quietly and kept licking and sucking my dick profoundly, making me consider pulling off onto the shoulder of the busy highway. *I'm the shit! I'm the shit! While I drive my dick get lick. I am the shit!* I sung to myself with confidence. I swerved slightly while readjusting my hands on the steering wheel and a white man in a red Corvette stared at me, smiling. He must've seen or detected what was going down inside my Acura. Toni's curly brown head could be seen bobbing up through the window slightly. I returned the smile and glanced down at Toni. The white man beeped his horn and signaled for me to pull over. I flipped him the bird and switched lanes, laughing at his perverted ass. The shift in lanes made Toni hesitate briefly and then resume without even questioning what had happened.

Having to pay too much attention to the road, I couldn't give my ejaculation my full concentration. Within fifteen minutes, we pulled onto Toni's block and I hesitantly obeyed her command.

"We're here," I announced, hardly able to speak coherently.

"Good, my jaws were lockin' up," she said and started rubbing her face. I left my penis hanging out until she ordered me to fix myself and get the bags outta the trunk.

"Are we going out tonight?" she asked me.

"Umm, yeah. Listen, let's go to Clemmy's tonight. Just for an hour or so, I have some business to handle. Please?" I asked her.

"Baby, I'm not the club type. I like lounges. Clemmy's has too much going on," she complained.

"Well, we're only staying for an hour. Come on, baby. Please, sweetheart, please?" I laid it on thick. She sucked in her teeth stubbornly.

"All right then. Hold on, I'll dress at your place then," she decided.

"Damn," I muttered to myself so she wouldn't hear me. I wanted to smoke while I was getting ready. "Okay," I said louder as I hauled the bags back into the trunk and we got back in the car.

* * *

Detective Taylor had briefed the three confident informers and gave them all their orders. They were to follow the brothers into the club and track their every move, observe anyone who was seen conversing with them, take note of their physical description, and attempt to observe any type of transaction between the brothers that may take place, all without being noticed.

"If they go to the bathroom, follow them. Act like you're just another customer using the john, too. If they go into the lounge area, get as close as possible. More than likely, they'll be the only white guys in there, so don't lose sight of them, no matter what. Understand?" she asked.

"No problem," the three narcs simultaneously agreed.

Taylor went on. "We'll be set up at the location of the vehicles transporting the brothers. We'll take it from there." Wollen and Bunning sat on the edge of the desk, staring stonily at the three informants. Both wore double shoulder holsters with pistols on both sides.

"We're counting on you'se guys to be very observant; they won't suspect any of you, so don't be afraid to get close to 'em. By God, that club holds fifteen hundred people!" Bunning encouraged them.

"Come on, let's go wait by their residence," Wollen suggested.

The three detectives got up and instructed the informants to wait on standby.

"We will call you when they leave. Make sure you stand right behind the brothers in the line. Listen to what they are talking about," Taylor told them one last time. They all agreed and the six of them departed.

* * *

Harold lay nodding off in the corner of the living room, waiting for Ronnie to pull up. He was supposed to be listening for the horn, but his strong high got the better of him. Drool dotted his chin, signaling the powerful trance the drug had put over him. He felt a kick and instantly regained consciousness and looked up, scared.

"Get your crackheaded ass up and out my house! Your dopey brother is blowin' the horn. Get out!" his mother yelled at him. A large Mexican man was waiting by the staircase.

"I'm sorry, Jose. These children of mine are strung-out heroin addicts," she apologized shamefully, leading the man up the stairs by the hand. Harold considered nodding back off, but this time he heard the horn and jumped to attention.

He ran outside, knowing a verbal beating was coming.

"What the fuck, asshole? You tryin' to miss out on the dope?" Ronnie screamed at him as he opened the door. They skidded off and headed toward I-83, which would take them to Charles Street. Ronnie was driving, which was a rare occurrence; he had neither the license nor the patience to drive a car.

"Here, Harold, you want some?" Jenny asked from the backseat, handing him a half pill of dope.

"No, I'll wait for the real shit. In minutes we'll have raw heroin to snort!" Harold said gleefully.

"I can't wait either!" Jenny agreed, excited. She withdrew her earlier offer and sniffed the pill herself.

* * *

Steve dabbed the last drops of Allure and patted down his 360-style waves. The fresh basketball jersey offset by the blue Air Force Ones looked and matched perfectly. He fitted the silver G shock watch and threw the white gold chain around his neck. He was ready to party. He picked up the phone and paged Cream. Seconds later, Cream called back, saying he was on his way.

Chapter 15

The music was deafening. We walked into the club hoppin', like real slick niggas. We didn't dance much, just stood in the corner with our mugs broke. Steve was either upset or jealous at the sight of Toni, for he didn't say one word the whole ride south. I was laced out in an Iceberg outfit and fresh black suede Timberlands. I was what you would call "shittin," if I do say so myself. Toni was my front; I had informed her en route to Steve's not to leave my side for any reason whatsoever. I probably sounded paranoid, but I refused to elaborate, just told her to stick to me like glue. I didn't under any circumstances want the brothers to see me, and Toni's presence would ensure that.

Steve clapped and hugged hands like he was a celebrity. It seemed he knew everyone in the packed club. He squeezed between Toni and I and whispered to me.

"Why did you bring her? She can't know what's going on."

"Man, I wasn't leavin' her at my crib. Besides, after we slide, we're going' on a trip," I told him.

"But shit might kick off when those white boys don't see no dope. Then what?" he asked, getting angry with me.

"Well," I seriously pondered, "we'll just have to get down. Fuck it. She here now," I told him as I felt Toni pulling me to the dance floor to dance to some stupid club song. She violently rubbed her donkey ass on my jeans with rhythm. I placed my hands behind my head and enjoyed the vertical lap dance until Steve interrupted.

"They're here!" The sight of the out-of-place white brothers and the scrawny white bitch they had in tow made butterflies creep into my stomach. I decided to stand up for myself.

"Yo, they *your* people. What you want me to do?" I asked Steve. "I don't want them junkies knownin' what I look like," and I really didn't. This conversation had broken Toni's rhythm and she stood there, staring at me. Steve rolled his eyes and headed toward the white boys. It must've been two hundred people staring at the white group, wondering what the hell they were doing there. I thought about what Steve said. He was right. I felt like I was sending him out alone to fight three people.

"Fuck it. Toni, stay right here or go dance with someone else right quick. I'll be right back," and I slid off to catch up with Steve.

I caught him just as he was shaking hands with the brothers. I recognized the white girl as Jenny, this bitch Steve had fucked in high school. It was obvious I was right in the way as they hugged. He pounded fists with Harold and offered Ronnie a shoulder tap. Harold held his hand out to me, but I chose to put my Iceberg shades on instead.

I ordered drinks for everyone and led the way to the lounge. The butterflies in my stomach made it nearly impossible to speak, and the brothers were impatient. Two busters kept lookin' nosily at my actions; they were so interested in my features I became annoyed.

"Mind ya fuckin' business, bitch! Da fuck you keep staring at?" I challenged them and tightened my grip on my Corona bottle in case of reciprocation. They responded with a noncommittal "fuck you" and disappeared. This brief test of balls gave me the courage to face the brothers, minus the butterflies.

"Now listen man," I said in my scariest voice, "the PO-lice pulled me over last night, saying that two brothers identified my car as one being involved in a murder. What the *fuck* is up with dat?" I lied to them.

"Fuck no. We don't even know you, or your car, so what the fuck you talkin' 'bout?" the younger brother growled.

Steve cut me off; sensing a riot was about to happen. "Hey Ron, right now we have thirty-five hundred cash; the dope is in the stash house. It's too hot to get it right now. We've been under investigation by the Feds for hustlin' and the murders made the heat rise," Steve lied.

He shut up when he noticed the two busters nosing into our conversation. His swift temper reacted quicker than usual and a stiff two-piece connected against one of their jaws. My anger, still boiling from the sparring earlier, blindsided the other one with the butt of my beer bottle. Blood shot out from his face onto my shirt and the sight of blood on my expensive shirt made me want to stamp the tongue out of his mouth, I was so angry.

Those fuckin' brothers set us up! I thought angrily to myself while I continued to kick the dogshit outta the nosy son of a bitch. This little skirmish drew an instant crowd. I felt myself being "L"ed out from behind, the bouncers slamming me hard on my chest, knocking the wind outta me. I noticed blood running from Ronnie's forehead and it appeared that someone had taken a parting shot at the white boy.

It took three bouncers and a can of pepper spray to get Steve off the nosy asshole. The helpless kid had apparently tried to rip off Steve's chain, which had made him snap even more. Steven's intention was to beat this guy into a seizure. Somebody tore Jenny's stretched shirt off and her braless pink titties bounced gingerly in the air. Harold had to be pulled out from under a crowd of angry patrons who had punched and kicked him relentlessly. The black partygoers had been waiting for a chance to beat up on the white boys, and the fight already in place had been all the invitation they needed.

My nose was bleeding badly from being dragged out the back door in a choke-hold by two bouncers. Steve had to be carried out, still fighting, his jersey ripped and his muscular chest scratched and bruised. Harold and Ronnie ran out, volun-tarily leaving Jenny behind, who nearly was being raped. Blood streaked her face from being slung around in the chaos. A gigantic bouncer was somehow able to free her and carried her out, occasionally feeling her naked breasts on the way.

They threw me out the door so violently that I landed on my back. The con-crete cut a huge gash in my left shoulder blade. Steve, who was almost blind from the pepper spray, called for water; blood decorated his upper torso.

Harold, Ronnie, and Jenny were nowhere in sight by this time, and the sharp pain in my shoulder made me forget about Toni.

"Come on, big guy. Let's go get some water over at that gas station. Let's just get some fuckin' water," I, who could barely stand myself, hoisted his two-hundred-plus-pound frame up and started limping toward the gas station.

We somehow made it and I ordered seven bottles of spring water so he could wash his eyes out thoroughly.

"And give me three Dutches," I added, sliding a ten-dollar bill through the glass. All I could think about was smoking this pain away.

My outfit was ruined, covered in blood, and Steve's brand new jersey was in shreds. We looked terrible. It was at this time that I remembered.

"Toni! Oh my God! Where's Toni? How did I forget her? Is she still inside? Fuck!" I yelled and took off, back toward the club. Steve was able to see after flush-ing his eyes out with five bottles of the water. He stopped me.

"Yo, them fuckin' brothers tried some shit on me, Cream," he was saying.

"What?" I hadn't caught that in the ruckus, I was too busy pounding the shit out of nosy-ass.

"Yeah, yo, he tried to steal me!"

"Who?" I asked, for I had seen no one tried to hit Steve.

"Ronnie! That's why his head got busted. Dem niggas in there wasn't gonna let no white boy steal me. He called me a nigger and said I stole his dope or some stupid shit like that. I'm gonna kill that bitch!" Steve said with conviction.

"Yo, those dudes were with them, I bet. You saw how they kept looking and coming real close to us. It was three of them, but one of them thought he was slick." I went on, "Man, that's disrespectful to mug a nigga while he talkin' busi-ness. That shit will get yo ass killed." My shades were crushed, my clothes were ruined, my girl was probably pissed, and we had two pissed-off dope fiends to deal with. *I can't fuckin' win with you, Steve,* I thought as I looked at him.

"Cream, baby!" someone cried out. It was Toni, thank God, coming around the corner. "My God, baby, what happened?" she worriedly asked.

"We got into a beef with some clowns that kept staring down my throat. I was just yellin' at 'em, but Steve hit one and it was on," I tried to explain to her. She tried to hug me, but she pressed against my hurt shoulder and I let out a sigh of pain, a grimace on my face.

"Ooooo, sorry, baby. Come on, let's go. The police are everywhere out front. They were putting some guy into an ambulance," she told me. I was glad I had parked two blocks away on Calvert Street.

I handed Toni the keys and helped Steve toward the car. His vision was still very blurry and the nigga couldn't see past then feet. We staggered on to the car and I helped Steve into the backseat and jumped in the passenger seat. Toni started it up and we took off.

"Take him to my house," I told her. "I can't send him home like this."

"Okay, sweetheart," Toni agreed. Knowing Toni, she probably wanted to play nurse with my body and eventually make love to my wounded flesh, but her hopes had been dashed with my invitation of Steve.

"Oh and, baby, don't be mad but I'm smokin' a blunt soon as I get home. I don't wanna hear no lip about it either," I forewarned her.

"Okay, I'll sit by the window so I don't have to smell it," she compromised. "Whatever you say, Daddy," she winked at me and I closed my eyes, hoping the throbbing pain in my shoulder would subside.

* * *

Ronnie couldn't decide whether to cooperate with the detectives now or later. He knew full well that his cut of dope had been sold.

"I told that nigger to bring my dope! He's fuckin' bullshitting me." His physical wounds were minute compared to his anger over his missing dope. "Thirty-five hundred? What the fuck is that? The dope would take a strong four! That's tripling the profit. We coulda made thirty-five hundred dollars off of just nine grams! That motherfucker better have thirteen or fourteen thousand!" Ronnie went on and on. No one else in the car spoke. They knew not to say a word when Ronnie got like this. He was deadly.

Harold, the most bothered of the trio, sat silently licking his wounds. He figured the brawl was a clever stunt on the part of Steve and his friend to avoid paying them the money. He knew involving the police would incriminate him and he wasn't going to jail for Ronnie or anyone else, dammit.

Jenny had luckily found a sweatshirt in the trunk of the car. Her feelings were hurt. She remembered her boyfriend leaving her in the mob of hands to free himself. She was almost raped because of his cowardice. Not only had she been violated but also betrayed by her boyfriend. Tears of pain, rage, and humility rained down from her eyes. Ronnie ranted on about Steve's believed disloyalty.

"He will pay. Big time. I'll call that fat bitch tomorrow morning and cop a deal." He was so angry he didn't think about the consequences this would have on himself and his brother. The remark about voluntarily going to prison was foolish.

"I tried to take his fuckin' head off!" Ronnie raged on and on, still pissed about his missing dope. A true fiend. He was a junkie who relied heavily on this upcoming dope and now he was fucked. "I only got forty fuckin' dollars! That won't last until noon. Then what?" he complained.

"I got a hundred, baby, we'll be fine for one more day," Jenny piped up from her daze. Her comments were well taken and Ronnie decided to relax a little. "Listen, Jennifer, I didn't mean to leave you but those fuckin' animals were out to kill me. I . . . I'm sorry I left you, okay? I was scared but if anything would have happened to ou, I woulda blown that whole fuckin' building up, I swear I would," he exaggerated.

Her heart was not open to his remorse. He had seen her nearly get raped, he had witnessed the mauling of her body. He watched her bare-breasted body being fondled by aggressive and cruel hands, and still he did nothing.

"I forgive you, Ronald," she lied, trying to sound sincere. She knew that if she would have revealed her true feelings, she would have caught a backhand across her face. One beating was enough for tonight, especially without any good blow to dull the pain.

* * *

The trio of detectives waited by the ambulance outside Clemmy's while the EMTs worked diligently. The guy inside the bus was unconscious and appeared to be suffering from a severe head wound. His head had been stomped repeatedly by heavy-duty work boots.

One informant was totally unharmed and ran to inform the detectives about what had gone down. The other narc suffered facial lacerations from the two-piece combination. He had lost a tooth in the battle and had a knot on his eye the size of a golf ball but had managed to retrieve the chain he had ripped from his attacker's neck. His swollen mouth altered his appearance drastically and his words were badly slurred.

One of the EMTs reported on the condition of the guy. "We're takin' him to Shock Trauma because of the head injury, but I think he'll be fine. They'll probably keep him a few days, though, just to be sure. He's got a deep laceration on his right cheekbone. Fragments of glass need to be taken out of the wound. He suffered a concussion so they'll do a CAT scan to see if there are any fractures or swelling of the brain. Off we go."

"Thank you," said Detective Taylor. Her plan had backfired badly. The amateur informants were detected and had the paint beat off their asses to prove it.

"I'm glad at least one of them is totally okay," she remarked. If this wasn't bad enough already, it soon became worse. The unharmed third informant spoke up.

"I didn't see no transaction. And the lighting in that place made it hard for me to get a good look at the guys they were talking to. I did hear the white girl mention something about dope, but it all happened so fast," he rushed on, his knees shaking. The sight of his bloody coworkers had scared the shit out of him. He could barely breathe when he was giving his report on the unfortunate events of the evening and his unsatisfactory performance. The truth was, as soon as he had heard the guy in the glasses threaten them, he hid under the table until the riot was already in full swing. He saw his friends being beaten and that's when he decided to make a run for it.

Chapter 16

It took three Dutches, a half pint of Remy Martin, and the warmth of Toni before I was able to slumber painlessly. Steve was sound asleep on the floor next to the dining room table.

I awoke to the sound of the TV. I rolled over and Toni was wide awake, lying there in my long white T-shirt. Her natural beauty was ravishing. I sat up and immediately felt stiff.

"How do you feel, troublemaker?" she asked me.

"I'm good. Glad to wake up to beauty," I told her.

"Yeah, well, I wasn't sure you would wake up at all after all them cigars ya'll sat up and smoke on. That shit stinks!" she remarked.

"Yo. To each their own. To me, it smells like the finest cologne," I jokingly told her, although I really did like the smell of marijuana.

"Baby, what about our trip? See?" She pointed to the bags and luggage that sat on the floor.

"We'll still go I just need to finish our business from last night. I promise," I assured her when I saw the look in her eye.

"Man, you're gonna get yourself killed. Why must you always 'finish business,' handle this, handle that? You've handled enough. Time to let it slide, baby." She lectured me as she got up and I caught a glimpse of her beautiful long brown legs. A flash of nastiness patrolled through my mind. Her body made my mouth water. When she returned with a cup of orange juice, I went to work sliding underneath the covers and came up inside of her shirt. She slightly resisted.

"Stop, bully, your friend is here." But she soon surrendered for my will was too strong.

"I only wanna kiss on Mommy, that's all," I whispered in between soft kiss-es. I slid her leopard skin thong off and began sucking on her clitoris like the

80

professional I was. She moaned softly, her secretions moistening her vagina. I liked licking the walls of her vagina aggressively and moved my tongue in and out of her pink pussy rapidly. Her wetness dripped down my mouth onto my chin as she squeezed my head violently between her legs. I continued sucking her clit until she breathed deep and began having an orgasm. I sucked until she pushed me away, shivering inside.

I wiped my mouth and went into the bathroom. The natural scent of her pussy made me search for the lotion and jerk my dick until ejaculation came. Drool hung form my mouth as come shot out and landed on the toilet seat.

After pleasing myself in privacy, I turned on the shower and stepped inside. *I wish that nigga would get out my house so I could get the real thing*, I thought to myself as the soap burned my open scrapes and cuts.

After leaving the shower and getting into fresh under clothes, I saw that Steve was awake.

"Dog, man, easy peace, what up?" he greeted with me his favorite saying and greeting.

"Hey speak easy, my neezy," I answered with my usual response.
"Hey, listen man, I just talked to my hopper and I gotta plan," he told me.

"Oh no," I groaned.

"No listen," he interrupted. "Check it. A move to prevent the brothers from going to the police." He told me about the plan he had devised. "I had my girl write an apology letter," he beamed with cleverness.

"From who?" I barked.

"From Sonny, retard!"

"Huh?" I was skeptical.

"Look, she's on her way over here. You'll see it," he promised.

"Whatever."

Toni had sneaked in during this exchange and stood looking at us like she was watching a tennis match. She had a dumbfounded look on her face as she stood in the doorway.

After fixing a wholesome breakfast of turkey bacon and pancakes for my guests, I head a soft knock at the door. I opened it to a fine-looking woman with skinny braids and a gold tooth.

"Hi. You must be Tanique," I guessed.

"Yup, where my boy?" She had the voice of straight ghetto. She marched in, thrust the note at Steve, and, after reading over it, he cracked up and handed it to me.

Ronnie,

I'm sorry for my treatment of you. I understand why you killed me.

I've enclosed $5,000 and 2 grams of the raw for you. Thanks for letting me pimp you all these years. My blood is on your hands 4-ever.

Your Dead Father,
Sonny

I looked at Steve in amazement. How could anyone be so stupid?

"They don't have to show this to the police," I deflated Steve. Toni wanted to see the note bad, but I quickly folded it up and handed it to Steve.

"Oh yeah, here, Boo. This all I could steal from my Baby Daddy," Tanique broke in with her ebonics and ghetto fabulous attitude. She removed a vial from the pocket of her tight jeans and handed it over to Steve. It had some kind of brownish powder in it.

"Look, Cream. The brothers will get the money, the dope, and the letter and figure that by accepting it, they're accepting the pay-off, which would make them more reluctant to go to the police. You dig?" Steve explained.

"I guess," I mumbled because I didn't dig it and I didn't want to talk about it with Toni there.

Steve got up, his chest covered with makeshift bandages. "Shorty gonna take me over there now," he said, and for once he hadn't involved me and my ride. "Hey, do me a favor. Give her two ounces of weed for me, for all her trouble getting the note and the vial for the brothers." I agreed with him and disappeared, coming back with the fifty-six grams of weed.

"I knew there was a catch somewhere," I said as I handed over the weed. Steve gathered up his battered body, killed the last of the cognac, hugged me, saluted Toni, and left.

A breath of fresh air consumed me when I heard the door shut. Thinking about the note, I muttered, "I thought he was only giving the brothers thirty-five hundred dollars." I guess his fear about the brothers going to the cops had made him up the offer.

Toni was staring at me stonily. "I want to know what the hell is going on right now," she demanded. I felt trapped, and after some brief consideration, I told her everything except the part about Pistol. She stared at me as if she had seen a ghost.

"I read about that in the newspaper. The girl committed suicide two days later. You're a murderer!" she screamed and took a few steps back from me.

"No, listen to me, Toni! I'm not," I tried to convince her as tears streamed down her beautiful face. I grabbed her and held her to me, all the while trying to defend myself against her accusations.

"I'm not!" I cried. "I'm not, Toni. I tried to stop him, you gotta believe me. Steve told me that the guy didn't have no guns, Toni. Please believe me!" I begged and cried into her hair. She continued to cry like a little girl who had just lost her best friend, and the sight of that combined with the truth of what had happened pierced my heart to the core. Toni tried to fight me off, but I refused to let her go. Instead I just held on to her tighter until I could feel her resistance break down.

When I regained control, I spoke softly and with remorse.

"Baby, I swear I didn't wanna have no part in this. Steve just asked me to watch his back; he said that nobody would get hurt. I know I'm wrong, I know. I never should have done this, baby, I'm sorry. But I didn't kill that guy. I want to get out of this so bad. I just wanna live with you, baby; I love you so much. Toni, please believe me. I want out! Everything! Selling drugs, smoking, drinking, everything! I want to live right by you, sweetheart." I said in a rush to her, but I meant

82

every single word. Finally, my words seeped through her and she began to kiss my hands and wiped my eyes.

"Baby, what are we gonna do? Huh? How are we gonna get you outta this?" she asked me and my heart melted with what she said next. "I believe you didn't want that boy dead, but you have to disassociate yourself from Steve. He's going to get you involved with this murder, I know it," she said to me. The thought of ending a fifteen-year friendship depressed me, but she had a point. If it weren't for him, I would never have been in Sonny's and watched the murders go down in the first place. But it was easier said than done since Steve was a part of my family.

* * *

Steve arrived at the large brown house at 2:28 P.M. Because he was a professional manipulator, he managed to talk Tanique into taking the note up to the front door.

"It's already sealed, with his name on it and everything. Just drop it in the mail slot," he told her. She did as he said and squeezed the bulging envelope through the mail slot and ran back to the car.

A shout came from the door, and when she looked back she saw an older white lady in a housecoat yelling obscenities at her and shaking her fist. She ignored the woman and jumped in the car.

"All right, take me home. I need a shower and a change of clothes," Steve told her, and Tanique started the car and pulled off. Then she fired up black 'n' mild, mixed with hydroponically grown marijuana. The creative concoction gave off a sweet smell and enticed Steve to take a drag. His head rushed after only one hit off the cigar.

"What's this?" he asked Tanique.

"I call it 'black weed.' My Baby Daddy put me on it. You take out half the tobacco and fill it up with weed. Shit you get high as hell, don't you nigga?" she explained as she took a long drag and passed it back to Steve.

"Yeah," Steve agreed. "What the hell is that? Sound like someone singing," Steve said and looked behind him.

"Nigga, you just geeking off this black. Ain't no one singin'," she laughed. She drove fast, for she knew her son's father would be home soon and there was no excuse for her not to be home to greet him.

She pulled into the driveway of Steve's beautiful house.

"Okay, baby, I gotta go. Damon is on his way," she told him. "Call me. Bye," she said as she sped off. Steve was walking to his front door when he heard screeching behind him. What the fuck?

"Get your fuckin' hands up, asshole!" a tall and slender black man screamed at him from behind. Steve turned around and saw five cop cars parked haphazardly on his beautiful driveway.

Detectives Bunning and Wollen jumped out of a police Suburban, guns drawn and aimed directly at Steve's head. Steve dropped to his knees. He had seen the suspicious-looking Suburban parked behind the house, but he never suspected it would be cops hiding in the bushes and grass.

Steve's mother, Mrs. Grovehand, had heard the confusion and came running out the front door, screaming, "No! No! No!" Bunning snapped the handcuffs on Steve's wrists, double locking them, and started to read him his rights.

At this same time Detective Taylor was sitting in an unmarked patrol car, twenty-five feet away. Ronnie and the third informant sat handcuffed in her backseat.

"Yeah, that's him. That's the guy from last night," said the informant excitedly. Ronnie sat morosely, watching the arrest. He then realized the familiar face next to him was one of the guys from last night. *Them bastards are good,* he thought to himself as he wondered about the repercussions of beating up the informants.

Ronnie sat uncomfortably in his handcuffs; they were biting into his wrists. He had not fully considered the consequences of his actions. He had made a rash decision to bring Steve to his knees, no matter what the cost, but had failed to realize that he, too, would have to spend years in jail for his own involvement. He remembered how Harold had refused to go with him and how he ran off to get high after Jenny brought back their six pills of scramble.

Detective Taylor didn't have to strike a deal with anyone. The brother had called her up, confessing to his involvement, and agreed to name and identify the shooter.

Steve considered resisting arrest, but the sight of his hysterical mother made him think twice.

"What the fuck did I do?" he asked the detectives repeatedly. Wollen ignored him and instead exercised his search warrant while Steve was hauled to the back of a marked cruiser.

When searching a residence for a murder weapon, the police often destroy the place in the process purposely. They made Steve's room look like it had had a visit from Hurricane Andrew. They recovered marijuana residue, three pills of Ecstasy, and a Swiss Army knife. They didn't find a pistol, ammunition, or large quantities of dope, marijuana, or cash.

Steve sat uncomfortably in the hot, smelly cruiser. He had been severely manhandled and the beating had left him hurting, for he was still recovering from the brawl the night before. After a lengthy search and ransacking, the two detectives and other numerous police officers came out of the residence. Bunning marched over to the car in which Steve sat and flung open the door.

"You're being charged with first-degree murder, attempted murder, false imprisonment, home invasion. Also, we're charging you with first-degree assault because of last night. And a cherry on top."

"Fuck you!" Steve spat. "I didn't kill nobody and ya'll bitches can't prove it, so shut the fuck up and take me in, bitch." With this he looked straight ahead and refused to look at Bunning any longer. Finally Bunning had met a mouth wiser than his own, but he was not to be outdone.

"Okay, big shot. Yeah, that's what they'll call your asshole. Big Shot!" He laughed rudely and slammed the door on Steve. He knew wise guys hated gay jokes and the look on Steve's face confirmed that Bunning had pissed him off.

Wollen sat waiting by the truck.

"Let's take him in and book him," Bunning said. "I can't wait to get that smart ass punk in interrogation." He was fuming. He banged on the hood of the cruiser.

As Steve was being led toward the police station, he could see a swarm of police surrounding Tanique's tiny car. She stood outside by the trunk, probably being questioned about her affiliation with Steve, and Steve thought that thankfully, he hadn't involved Cream in this one.

Chapter 17

Toni lay peacefully beside me, her light snoring signified the past few days of mental and physical exhaustion I had put her through. I had a funny feeling in my heart but could not put my finger on its origin. I stared at the neatly packed luggage in the corner; a trip was definitely in order to erase the pain in my troubled life. The mental anguish and spiritual stress was mounting by the day. Instead of things getting better, they had only gotten worse, and it was something that was bothering me immensely.

My cell phone rang and it was Mrs. Francis. I decided to allow my voice mail to pick it up. I was in no mood to do business, although I had no idea why. I gathered myself and tiptoed past Toni, hoping that I didn't wake her. I went into the desolate kitchen, where I had stored the weed and the money. I removed the large trash bag in which I'd been dispensing weed. The once twenty pounds now looked more like leftovers and the trash bag was half-empty. Thousands of seeds were gathered at the bottom of the bag and I briefly entertained planting the wild seeds. "Nah," I laughed.

My shoulder began to throb; the effects of the pain-relieving Cognac and weed had worn off. I immediately ingested two extra-strength aspirins and washed it all down with a half cup of orange juice. I reached into the trash bag and grabbed a handful of weed and put the bag in the safe. I got a Dutch from the box I kept on the counter and crept into the bathroom.

I quickly sliced the cigar and removed the guts. I licked the entire outer leaf; it was kind of stale, while I sprinkled the grounded ganja inside. I quickly sealed my creation with a roll and a lick, which I personally called "kissing the blunt."

Anxious to sneak past Toni, I only slipped on some slippers and shorts and bolted out the door. My chest was aching and bruised, and I picked up a city newspaper and walked toward the Dumpster, stepping off to light the cigar. I smoked looking around all paranoid for the weather was seventy degrees and people were sitting on both sides of the street. I was so sullen. *Why am I so sad?*

I thought the buzz would relieve my depression, but I had no such luck. The high was semi relaxing me but not very joyful. It seemed as if someone watched my every move.

I discontinued my smoking and began walking toward my building. A violent head rush overtook me and I felt like I was about to pass out. The mixture of the extra-strength aspirin with the drugs sent a dizzying sensation through my body. I felt as if I was about to throw up from being spun around on a Ferris wheel.

Upon entering the apartment, Toni was staring desolate at the floor. Tears were running down her face.

"What's wrong, baby?" I asked her gently.

"Who the fuck is Treesy?" she asked. Shit! In such a rush to sneak outside and smoke, I had forgotten to take my cell phone. Some dumbass chickenhead had called my phone, and Toni, feeling secure, had answered it, I guessed.

"She just someone that buys weed," I lied.

"Bullshit, Donny. The bitch said she fucked you twice, Nigga, she described everything! Your apartment! Your body! Your car! Fuckin' everything!" Toni yelled at me.

"I know. She came over to buy some weed and asked to see my tattoos. Then her ride left her, so I gave her a ride to the bus stop. I swear," I lied some more.

"Bitch, you're lying. Listen, Cream. I ain't gonna be played by you. Fuck that. You already got one kid by a girl you ain't with and I ain't gonna be the second," she told me, and I believed her.

"Man, fuck Treesy. She lying 'cause she jealous of you. She don't even know me or nothing about me so she's fuckin lying."

My cell phone rang again and Toni snatched it up before I could.

"Who dis? . . . Christina? What? . . . How you know him? . . . Oh, you fucked him and sucked his dick the other day . . . okay. Hey, you white or something? . . . I thought so. Well bitch, you can have this lying muthafucka," she told Christina and hung up. A look of utter disbelief covered my already pale face. How the fuck could I be caught twice in five minutes? Because I was high, my words just tumbled out of my mouth and I stuttered furiously while Toni dressed in a hurried rage. The remnants of my buzz made my sincerity hard to express.

"Toni, baby, you're not leaving. Yeah, I do know those girls, but I ain't fuckin' none of them. That white girl fucks with Steve. He used to give her my phone number to try and brush her off. Why didn't you ask her what I looked like?" I made this seem so logical I half believed it myself. Toni paused for a minute and then grabbed the phone again, no doubt to hit redial and call Chrisina back. Hurriedly, I snatched it from her and continued my plea.

"Look, Toni, you must believe me. I only want you." The thought of that fat white girl putting salt in my game pissed me off and hurt me at the same time.

I began to stutter my words, a further sign of my guilt and intoxication. The phone rang, but Toni didn't answer it this time and neither did I.

"Two is enough for me," she muttered and stood up. She started sorting out her luggage, as if she was ready to take the vacation by herself.

"Toni, please. Wait. I love you." I tried to cry, but I was too high still to make them come. The more somber I tried to sound, the faster she packed her shit, it seemed.

"Cream, everything happens for a reason. Just like it was meant for me to find out about your involvement with those murders. It was meant for me to see you playing with all that weed this morning when you thought I was asleep. I saw you creep past me with no shirt on, you fiend," she told me in a calm voice. "I was just thinking about your sneakiness when your phone rang and kept on until I finally got tired of listening to it and answered it. And what do I find? Some skank saying she dates you and fucks you off and on. I was waiting for your ass to come back in here. I saw you, slumping down by that Dumpster to smoke. You think you're so slick!" She kept on and on. "Then you come back in here and another bitch calls the phone." I tried to break in and defend myself but a wave of her hand shut me up.

"Then another bitch calls," she repeated, not about to be interrupted. "This time, a white girl who says you made her suck your dick then disappeared while she dozed off." Tears of pain and hurt streaked her beautiful face and I could see her pain. "Cream, I'm sorry, but I gotta go. Have a good life."

I was in shock, numb with pain and emotion. I sat in a trance, my eyes fixed to the spot at which Toni stood to give her speech, and my daze was only broken by the sound of the front door slamming shut. The loud thud signified the finality of Toni's words.

I sat frozen, wanting to go after her but realizing soon that my idea was useless. Toni was gone forever. I wanted to die as a feeling of complete despair racked my body. Finally, the tears mounted and flowed freely. When it rains, it pours.

Chapter 18

I woke with a painful kink in my neck. It was nearly impossible to turn my head to the left. I had managed a good nap, despite all my troubles and woes, and I lay looking at the wall, considering my plans for the evening.

I reached into my shorts and removed the half piece of blunt that had cost me my relationship with Toni. My earlier headache was alleviated, thanks to the aspirin and the hour-long nap.

Before sparking the blunt, I decided to call Toni to express my deep regrets for my actions and to try to convince her of my remorse and to come back. It had been only four hours since the argument, but I hoped she had begun to cool off and forgive me.

I dialed her number, only to hear the operator say it's been changed to an unpublished number. What? That quick? Toni was obviously not in the mood for a make-up. She must've gotten the number changed as soon as she left my place. I thought it usually took twenty-four hours but remembered that Toni's father worked for the phone company. She was probably able to get immediate action because of his name.

The pain began to creep back into my soul. I couldn't fathom losing Toni forever. I never contemplated the consequences of my infidelity. Actually, it had been me who had suggested that we commit to each other and Toni had agreed happily before making her sweet love to me. At the time it was only a clever ploy to ensure house pussy. I knew that what I was about to do were the actions of a dog, but I couldn't stay up and agonize over the loss of Toni all day and night. Her voluptuous buttocks made doggy-style pure ecstasy. I had become pussy whipped and selfish and wanted Toni to feel obligated to fuck only me. The actual dedication of a relationship wasn't given much thought. I had only thought about the great sexual experiences that we enjoyed together.

As I sat thinking about the last time we made love, my penis became throbbing hard until I couldn't take it anymore. Sex was dominating my mind. I picked up the phone and called Carolina, a girl from down south that was a freak for hire. The beauty in Caroline was that she lived within walking distance of me.

Her chocolate-brown complexion and five-foot, eight-inch frame made her sexy in her own little way.

"Hey, wuz up? This Cream," I politicked on the phone for a few more minutes until the arrangement was made. She told me her rates real quick before hanging up.

"Fifty for some pussy, seventy-five for some head and pussy, and a hundred for the works." I chose the fifty-dollar package, for I'm considered to be tight pockets when it comes to females.

As if she had been sitting there waiting for me to schedule an appointment, Carolina popped over a short ten minutes after we hung up. I took my .380 from the safe and laid it in plain view, in case she was contemplating robbing me. I gave her Grant's face and loosened my pants. She went into the bathroom and came out stark naked within three minutes. She held her clothing and sandals in her hands until I told her to drop them.

My dick was limp and I attempted to wax her into sucking it on the house.

"No, Cream. Twenty-five dollars," she told me. She did allow my penis to touch her lips but would not unlock her mouth, teasing me. I became frustrated and aggressive and forced my dick into her mouth by grabbing the back of her neck and forcing her mouth open.

"I'll pay the fuckin' twenty-five bucks. Just suck it, bitch," I said. I continued to jam my groin into her lips until I could feel her tongue massaging my penis. I could feel the tension releasing with her every lick and kiss, and finally my penis disappeared into her mouth.

The victory by force sent a soothing sensation throughout my body. This girl had skills enough to suck a golf ball through a water hose. My phone rang loudly and broke my peaceful trance, but she continued sucking while I rearranged myself to reach it.

"Hello?" I answered.

"It's Toni. I left some stuff over at your place. I'm out front. Can you get my bag from the bathroom and run it down for me?"

"Ummmm . . . no. I'm busy right now," I stuttered.

"Doing what?" Toni demanded.

"Nothing. I mean, Toni, I have to go." God, this was awful. "Don't come up. I won't answer the door. I'm in no mood to see you right now," I lied.

"Nigga, bring my shit!"

"No. I'll give it to you later."

Carolina had stopped sucking now and said as clear and loud as she could: "That's all I'm doin' for free now, Cream." Jesus Christ! I frantically motioned for her to shut up, but the damage had been done. I heard a deafening scream through the phone and then a stream of hysterical crying. I then heard the phone hang up and tires screech off. I peeked out the blinds and saw Toni's small car disappearing down the block.

The new phone number had thrown me off. I thought it was a potential sale. I hit End, put the phone down, and slapped Carolina hard across the mouth.

"You dumb bitch! I told you to shut up!" I don't know what had become of me; I had turned into some kind of uncontrollable monster. I had never put my hands on a woman before and the blood dripping from her mouth only brought more shame.

I grabbed the terrifed and hurt Carolina, turned her over, and forced my half-limp penis into her anus. I pumped her hard until the juices began flowing again. Carolina begged me to fuck her in the ass with all my force.

"Fuck me, Daddy! Mommy was a bad girl. Fuck my asshole hard, Daddy!" she cried out. I continued ramming my penis into her much-visited anus. A demonic rage filled my soul—I was so tired of the bad luck and misfortune that had come to me. I was beginning to feel like I was cursed. I withdrew my penis and jammed it into her soaking wet pussy. I thought about how we weren't using any protection as her raw insides pleasured me. I continued to fuck her gaping hole, ignoring my conscience, until I felt myself ejaculating. My attempt to pull out was futile, and come shot into her vagina at full force. She lay down with delight, the warmth of my semen confirming that she had done her job well. I nestled next to her briefly, panting like an out-of-shape track runner.

When I felt my energy emerge again, I peered at the dry blood that had come from my assault to her face. She lay next to me, scared to move unless ordered. I grabbed the half blunt and sat up on the bed, staring at my victim with fear in my heart. The vile actions to her anus left an orange secretion on her leg. Her slender frame was marred with stretch marks from the three children she had born out of wedlock.

"Go spark this blunt for me," I told her and handed it to her. She jumped up and obeyed me and returned in seconds with the fiery stick in her hand. I removed the blunt and got up to replace the pistol in the safe and get thirty dollars.

To her surprise, I was paying what I owed her and then some, but it was really out of my guilt of hitting her. I threw the money on the bed.

"Here. But you're going to fix me up better, ain't you?" I asked and she nodded. "Yeah, I know. Thirty dollars worth of head feels better than that," I told her and she put her face to my groin. I didn't even wash the juices from her rectum off my balls, and a disgusting feeling came over as I watched her put my shitsoaked dick into her mouth.

I reclined back and smoked my cheeba, my mug broke and my mind racing. I was barely even paying attention to Carolina's attempt to please me.

When I was finally satisfied, I scolded her. "Now get up and go wash ya face, shit mouth." I didn't want her leaving my apartment with dried blood all over her mouth. I bizarrely thought of being blessed with a blood mouth, and even weirder, it turned me on. My mind was becoming evil.

She dressed quickly and waited for my direction. I stared back at her with eyes of stone. "Carolina, get the fuck out," I told her and motioned toward the door. In my opinion, she had spoken loudly out of spite; she knew I was talking on the phone with a female, one I was attempting to avoid. Her amplified tone of voice served as her amusement for the day. I paid her balance to avoid vengeance on her part. An unpaid hooker could not be trusted.

I smoked the roach until it burned my fingertips. I was sitting there, French inhaling the smoke, when my phone rang.

"Hello," I answered grimly, not in the mood to talk to anymore. It was Steve's mother, crying, saying that Steve had been arrested for murder earlier that morning. The phone fell from my hands as my world went black.

* * *

Bunning, Wollen, and Taylor all took turns trying to bring Steve to a confession. Steve sat looking at the magic mirror, smoking a cigarette and ignoring them. The lure of a cop-out didn't faze him because he knew that without a gun and witnesses, a guilty verdict would be slim; murder is one of the hardest charges to prove without solid evidence. He knew that his parents had the money to afford the best attorney in the city.

He pictured the trash bag full of weed sitting over at the white girl's house and laughed. He had covered all his tracks.

Bunning reentered the interrogation room and sat so close to Steve that Steve's arm brushed his leg while he was swinging it nonchalantly.

"We know you killed them people. We know you killed Sonny. But man, it was self-defense and you'll walk. We just want you to tell us what happened so we can nail the white boys," Bunning tried to conjole Steve into snitching.

Steve laughed. "Man, Maryland ain't got no self-defense statute. Who you fooling? It don't matter, though, because I didn't kill nobody brother." Steve saw the black batting gloves that Bunning was squeezing his fat hands into and butterflies crept into his stomach. He knew the room was being watched, and the second he got the better of the black cop, he would be outnumbered greatly and probably charged with assaulting a police officer. Bunning was smaller than Steve but in much better physical shape because Steve was a heavy smoker. However, Bunning knew that this young buck would give him a run for his money so he had to act fast.

He grabbed Steve up by the front of his shirt and slammed him against the wall. Steve's tender wounds from the night before were aggravated and he let out a little sigh of pain.

"Listen, you fuckin' punk. You can act all cool and slick if you want, but if we find one strand of forensic evidence from you in that apartment, your ass will rot in prison," Bunning promised and unexpectedly kneed Steve in the groin then pushed Steve on his face. He stood over him, his eyes bulging and his veins popping.

"Tell me what happened!" he screamed. At that time, Wollen entered the room while Steve lay crouched on the floor, hissing in pain.

"Fuck you, Bunny!" Steve said through clenched teeth. Steve's play on Bunning's name infuriated him, and he kicked Steve viciously until Wollen cut in.

"Easy there, Henry. Give the guy a chance to breathe."

92

Bunning relented and left the room. It was the good ol' good cop/bad cop routine. Usually a suspect would confide in the cop who was nice to him, who "saved" him.

"You all right, man? That fucking Bunning is tough as nails. Here, let me help you back into the chair," he offered and a glass of water was produced. Steve drank while Wollen lit a cigarette. After he had downed the water, he grabbed a cigarette from the pack Wollen was offering and inhaled deeply. Wollen continued.

"Listen, man. We have a guy saying you killed someone, possibly two people. The brother, you know. Now we have another three guys who can identify you negotiating numbers with the brothers at Clemmy's. Wanna tell me what ya'll was talking about?" Wollen asked solicitously.

Steve was restless and paranoid after learning he had been spied on at Clemmy's. He figured the brothers had been working with the cops from the door. Recalling how he had left the now apparent spy, Steve said slowly to Wollen, "Me and Ronnie's been friends for years. I fucked his girlfriend while he was in rehab and he found out. I told him that didn't want any trouble and offered to settle the feud with some cash. Only he didn't want cash, he wanted dope because he said that his connect had gotten killed and he was needing some. So I told him to meet me at the club and I'd give him two grams of dope," Steve said.

"Where did you get the dope?" Wollen asked.

"I sell it every now and then; I had some stepped-on shit left over from a bundle. Anyway, we met at the club and some asshole kept staring at my friend."

"What friend?"

"A friend from the club. I can't remember his name. But the guy kept staring at us and I asked him why. He said 'fuck you' and then I went off 'cause I have a real bad temper," Steve explained. He was trying to throw the truth and fiction together.

"What about Pistol? Where is he?" Wollen asked. *Those fucking brothers told everything!* he thought with anger; he was flustered.

"I don't know where Pistol is," he lied. He was so glad that he had not mentioned Pistol's origin or real name to Ronnie. He had originally wanted to but had forgotten to bring it up to him before the heist. Ronnie had only asked for a description of the front buyer.

Wollen jotted down everything Steve said and Steve suddenly remembered his right to remain silent and decided to exercise it before he incriminated himself or was caught up in a lie.

"Mr. Wollen," he started innocently, "I understand that everything I say can and will be used against me; therefore, I am going to remain silent and request an attorney before I speak again."

"I see," Wollen said and looked at Steve strangely.

Steve was escorted into the bullpen. He would spend the night inside a holding cell and then be transported to Kelso Drive for a bail review.

He was puzzled, wondering how long he had been followed and spied on. Were the brothers connected to the police? Were they wired? He thought about how he was at the brothers' house earlier today and the note. Then he thought about Tanique. He hoped she didn't spill any information about the note.

He recalled the grim night of the murder, so entrenched with the reward for the caper that he didn't realize he was risking his own life, too. He had never stopped and realized that he had killed a man until the police shouted it at him. Recalling the charge papers made him worry. The sight of the word *murder* right next to his name was hard to take. He had simply viewed it as heroics, saving both himself and his friend from being hit with the humongous gun. He had never accepted the blame in his mind until the detectives explained it to him.

He had gone into an occupied home and killed a man out of sheer greed. It was all starting to hit him, looking at the prison bars. He prayed that God would make a way.

"I'm sorry, Lord. I just didn't want the guy to kill us. I'm sorry," he weeped softly.

Chapter 19

I woke up at 4:26 A.M. It was Tuesday, March 14. I lay naked on my floor with the phone still beside me. For some reason, I would almost go into a coma when deeply stressed.

The initial shock had worn off and I began to wonder how Steve was doing. I hoped he had covered all his tracks. I cried as I thought about our situation, tears flooding my eyes like a reopened wound.

I sat up looking at the wall with a depressed look of a tired man on my face. The pressure had mounted to the point of destruction. I knew not how much more my fragile mind could handle.

I tried to piece together a version of what happened in my mind. The brothers must have told the police; the police probably saw Steve drop the money and note off and followed him home. They apparently locked him up before he walked in the door. I breathed deeply. I was so reliant on drugs my brain felt strange when sober. I twisted open the bottle of vodka and took a long swallow. I let the alcohol drip from my lips onto my hair chest. The strong liquor made me choke, resisting the swallow of the undiluted firewater. I was hungry, for it had been nearly sixteen hours since I had eaten anything.

My body began rejecting the alcohol, and mouthfuls of saliva watered my beard and chest. I was basically just sitting there, spitting all over myself. I didn't know the specifics of Steve's situation, but the possibility of my best friend never seeing daylight made me feel as though it was me in prison. My stomach twisted in a knot, and I attempted to stand. I became nauseated and dizzy as I tried to walk. My stomach suddenly erupted and vomit shot out of my mouth like I was possessed. I rushed to the kitchen sink, the closest thing, picturing the rotting body of Pistol. I continued to regurgitate all over the dirty dishes in the sink until I choked on my own saliva.

Tears streaming down my face, I clung to the kitchen sink for support, spittle hanging from my mouth. My head throbbed, my stomach ached, and my body cried for some peace. I regained my composure and a slight odor invaded my nostrils.

I stumbled back into my bedroom and turned on the light. An orange fluid stained my sheets and stuck to my penis. Crusty shit was all over my balls. A strong body odor permeated the air and I figured its cause was Carolina, the hooker I had hired. I had neither changed my sheets nor washed my body.

Although I suffered no injury to my legs, I limped badly to the stash box and removed the marijuana; a little relief filled me when I saw it. I staggered back to my bed and lay on top of the crusty sheets. My brain was on the brink of a total meltdown.

I somehow managed to roll a Dutch and slid off the bed to light my creation. I used the pilot light on the stovetop and watched as the blue flame ignited my blunt. I inhaled deeply and instantly my stomach felt queasy; I somehow forced the vomit to stay down and warded off the dry heaves. I pulled hard on the Dutch, which caused it to run, when one side of the cigar burns faster than the other. Probably because of my half-assed rolling job, I suspected. I spit on my finger and stopped the run as best as I could and resumed my toking.

I walked back to the bed and collapsed on the unsanitary sheets. Hygiene was the last thing on my mind at this point. The reefer did its job and relaxed me, but it also made me cry from the years of memories Steve and I had shared. I used one of my tears to prevent another run, pulling hard on my homemade cigar. I held in the smoke as long as I could because I wanted to experience the full dose. My stomach became tight and I hunched over to relieve the ache slightly. No matter how intense the pain, I continued smoking the weed.

My subconscious piped up and told me to get the weed away from me, but I discounted the notion as simple paranoia. I felt like going into the bathroom and lying in the tub with the water on full blast and praying to wake up in heaven. My scary thoughts of going to jail for murder scared the shit out of me. I just couldn't believe my best friend was in jail for something we had worked so hard to cover up. I started to pound myself on the head repeatedly. My conscience was screaming at me.

You known better!
You are so stupid!
You are going to jail!
You should have sat your black ass home!
You're going to jail for murder because you are stupid!

I couldn't take it anymore and I screamed to God in heaven to save me. Tears of pain and frustration soiled my face. I smoked the weed, crying and coughing at the same time, staring at the ceiling.

The high was powerful and it brought me back into perspective. I said aloud to my conscience, "I'm not going anywhere. They can't take me for murder; I didn't kill anyone. Besides, the white boys don't know me, so stop fuckin' crying like a bitch." It was time to scold myself. I tried, but the tears kept flowing.

I was truly hurt that my best friend was in jail for a crime that I had taken part in. It was my fault. The devil on my right side tried to convince me not to worry about Steve. The angel on the other side told me to repent, for I had sinned greatly, and to get rid of the possessions acquired from the robbery and run into the house of the Lord and beg forgiveness. I listened to both as I continued smoking. I knew my mind was playing tricks on me.

I became drowsy and barely held my head up straight. The combo of the weed, the tears, and the early hour of the morning overwhelmed my already stressed out body and mind. I took my pillow and lay underneath my dining room table, and within minutes, and typical of my habits, I was deep asleep.

* * *

The ringing of the phone awakened me. It was 11:34 A.M. and the sun was shining brightly through my windows. I grabbed the phone and hurriedly answered it with a rushed "hello."

"Hi, Donny. It's Mrs. Grovehand."

"How's Steve?" I asked her right off.

"Well, not good," she responded. "He went to the bail hearing this morning and they denied his bail. He'll probably have to sit in jail until the court date, is what the lawyer says." My love for Steve was evident, for I was truly upset by this news.

"But how can they deny his bail? He didn't do anything," I protested. "They are framing him 'cause they need to get someone for it."

"I know, baby, I know. I talked to Steven last night and he said it's that white boy Ronald that's been lying on him because of that Jennifer. Lawyer says they don't have a case and should be fine, but he wants fifteen thousand dollars for it and we're gonna need some help with that." With this, she burst into tears, muttering about her "baby boy, sweet precious baby boy."

Steve had an older sister who married some Frenchman and moved to Paris thirteen years ago. Steve has basically been an only child for the past thirteen years. I couldn't imagine how she felt.

"We went to the final hearing. He said to tell you to come over between two and five and he'll call to give you instructions," she went on.

"Yes, ma'am," I said. Then I said something out of character. "Please pray for us, Mrs. Grovehand. We all need it."

"Bless your heart, son," she cried into the phone.

"I'll bring five thousand over around three, you know, to help out with Steve's lawyer and all," I told her.

"That would be great, baby,"

"See you then," I said and I hung up.

I was feeling so much better than I had earlier, and the words of the lawyer rejuvenated my depressed spirit. Maybe there was some hope after all. I still needed to be cheered up, so I decided to dedicate my day to my true joy and inspiration: my son, Daniel.

I called them up and immediately put my bid in for some quality time.

"Daddy, you comin' get me?" my two-year-old asked.

"Yep. I'm on my way," I promised him and hung up. I put on a pair of sweat-pants and a T-shirt with no socks or underwear and slipped my feet into my house slippers and rolled out of my apartment for the first time in nearly two days.

I drove and wondered about my future in the drug business. What would it take for me to get out of the game? *Nothing*, my conscience replied.

I pulled into the townhouse complex to pick up my son, who was waiting anx-iously outside with a lunchbox and a book bag. My baby mama stood inside the door, watching him, and a bald head could be seen through the reflection of the upstairs window.

"Still freakin'," I laughed to myself as I circled the block. She knew that I was going to have to get the carseat, and she chose that time to bother me about other bullshit.

"When you gonna buy a carseat? You got money, Mr.Big-time Weed Dealer," she said nastily to me.

"When you gonna buy a car, Miss Big-time Dick Sucker?" I shot back. I was in no mood for her mouth. I put my son in the front seat and strapped on his seat belt.

"When you bringin' him back?"

"Umm . . . never. Psyche! Thursday or Friday probably," I told her and couldn't believe she was really going to let me drive our son around in the front seat without a carseat. What a dirty motherfucka.

My son was my heart, but because of the ill relationship I had with his mom, it was hard to show it. His mother was a one-night stand turned whole life plan, and I truly didn't know anything about her or what I was getting into having a baby as a teenager. She made my life miserable when given the chance, and it caused me to stay away. I knew this affected my relationship with Daniel.

Daniel wasn't used to riding in the car very often, especially nice ones. After ten straight minutes of giggling and looking around and checking things out, he was sound asleep. The apartment was a mess, so I decided to take him to see his grand-mother for an hour or so. I saw my mother's car parked out in front of the house and I was relieved. I was surprised she wasn't at some church service or something.

Daniel woke up when the car stopped moving and I rushed him out of the door to avoid hearing my mother's mouth about the dangers of not having a carseat. I used my spare key and went inside and saw my mother sitting at the table smoking a blunt. Good. I really needed to smoke.

I took the bud while she hugged Daniel and asked him tons of questions that he couldn't answer. We sat and conversed for a minute and I told her about Steve while Daniel played with some leftover toys he had found.

"I'll pray for him and put his name on the altar," she promised.

We talked for an hour or so more and I decided to go home. It was almost 6:00 P.M. by this time, and even though I had missed Steve's call, I wanted to arrange the money drop off the next morning.

"Won't you let me keep the baby until tomorrow?" my mother asked.

"I just got him today, Ma. How about you get him tomorrow night?" I compromised.

"All right," she agreed, and we left. I was hoping she wouldn't walk us to do the door, but she did and she yelled, "Boy, go get a carseat. You got money?"

We pulled off and headed home for the evening. I would put the baby to bed after dinner, clean the house, and sort out how much weed would need to be sold to compensate my man's lawyer.

I entered the house that looked more like the aftermath of a rumble and immediately saw the filthiness of the place. I was second-guessing bringing my young son to see such a horrible site. *Thank goodness he's sleeping*, I thought as I laid him down on the dining room table so I could change my bed linens.

I replaced the sheets, comforter, and pillowcases and laid Daniel down on my queen-sized bed, still fully dressed with the exception of his shoes and socks. I went into the bathroom and rolled a blunt while taking a shit. *My customers are probably cursing me out*, I thought to myself. It had been close to two days since I had responded to calls. I flushed the toilet and ran the water. I was going to take a relaxing bath and sit in the tub to smoke my Buddha. Then I was going to clean up the atrocious apartment.

I relaxed into the steaming hot water and lit the El, finally able to come back around.

Chapter 20

At 4:30, the Northeastern District received an anonymous phone call. The caller, who refused to identify themselves, offered a tip as to the whereabouts of a large cache of drugs. The officer responding to the call immediately called the drug task force and transferred the caller to a detective.

"Hey, Harvey. How can I help you?" the detective answered when he picked up the line.

"No, actually I can help you," replied the informant. "I know where a lot of drugs are being hidden and I feel it's detrimental to my environment."

"Well, I couldn't agree with you more. Wanna give me some more information on the exact location or the guys?" the detective eagerly asked.

"Yeah, sure. His name is Donny Wise and his address is 5015 Goodnow Road, apartment J. His license plate number is GTX-300. That's all I can tell you, but I want something done now before the drugs are moved." The caller was a wealth of information.

"What kind of drugs?"

"Crack, heroin, weed, a coupla machine guns, whatever. It doesn't matter, but I can assure you it will be well worth your time, officer," the informant promised.

"Well, now, see, since we don't know anything about this guy yet, it will be hard to get a warrant tonight."

"You'll have to call in a favor then."

"You'll have to escort us to the judge and swear before him that your allegations are, without a doubt, totally accurate. You'll have to agree that if nothing is recovered you'll be arrested for perjury. Do you understand all this?" The detective had a plan.

"Yeah, no problem," answered the confident informant. "If nothing is found, go ahead and lock me up. But I am a hundred percent sure that's not gonna happen. So where should we meet?"

"I'll call a judge and we'll have to meet privately in his chambers. How about this? You meet me at the Northeastern Police Station, and by then, I'll have contacted a credible judge," the detective, Harvey, said.

"I'm on my way," answered the informant and the phone went dead.

* * *

I had just finished cleaning the hell out of my apartment and the hard work had left me exhausted. The baby had eaten and was sound asleep. Looking at him made me smile to myself. My phone rang and it was just a few customers asking for my whereabouts.

"Just chillin'," I answered, "but I'm in for the night. I'll holla at ya tomorrow. I got my seed here with me," I told them, looking at Daniel. The phone rang again as soon as I had hung up with the last call. This time it was my brother.

"Hey, nigga. We havin' a cookout. Come through," he invited me.

"Naw, I'm beat, Mo. I got Dan, so I'm just gonna to post up for the night," I told him.

"Yo, nigga want a quarter pound. Come get that money," he tried to persuade me.

"Oh, ya'll doin' it like that?" I teased him. "But, bro, I'm chillin'. Catch me on the rebound and I'll treat you to lunch at the Factory," I told him.

"All right, den. Holla back," he said and I hung up the phone. I probably would have jumped up and done it if it weren't for the baby being asleep. *Fuck it, can't make every party*, I thought to myself as I lay next to my baby, his soft breathing full of innocence. Being next to him made me comfortable. I grabbed him closer and snuggled him tightly and dozed off, snoring loudly and drooling all over my fresh linens.

* * *

A loud-ass bang on the door woke me up out of my peace. The room was pitch black and I wondered what the hell was going on. I thought I was dreaming until the bang got louder and more obvious.

Annoyed, I yelled out, "Who is it?"

"The police," they screamed back, and about that time, the door splintered at the weight of their police-issued battering ram. Within seconds my tiny apartment was flooded with men dressed in black with shields and guns.

"Get on the floor!" someone screamed at me and I followed their instructions. It was at this time I saw a pistol aimed toward my son. I started shaking with a volcanic anger and I was ready to erupt. Quickly, someone put me in handcuffs and plastic restraints around my ankles and sat me up in a chair. Every light in the apartment was turned on, and for the first time I saw Drug Task Force written on the back of their jackets. My mind couldn't calculate what was going on. Was this for the murder or what? Why were all these cops going through my small studio apartment?

"What's going on, officer?" I asked one of the cops, terrified.

"We got a tip from one of your friends that said it might be well worth our time to come over here and check you out. Personally, we didn't even know you existed, but we got a good tip and we're just doing our job," a fat black cop named Harvey answered me.

"Here it is! In here!" another cop called out excitedly. A blond female cop came up to Harvey and told him, "I got it," and she pulled a large trash bag out from behind her and opened it so everyone could see that it was full of marijuana. Everyone in the room started to smile except me. Daniel, thank God, was still sleeping.

"We got a combination safe," someone said.

"Drag it downstairs and bust it open any way you can," Harvey ordered. An older white man pulled up a chair.

"Now listen, son. I have good news for you. We're going to give you the chance to work with us. If not, you're going to jail, my man. Tell us where you got the weed. Just set us up like someone did you, and I will guarantee you'll walk with only probation," he told me.

"Man, fuck you. I ain't snitching on nobody," I coldly said to him. "I got the weed from a drug strip over in West Baltimore. I bought that whole bag to smoke. Just me. I don't wanna involve no one else. Just me," I told him and crossed my arms over my chest. The bitch cop tried to provoke me.

"You sure 'just you'? Your son's sleeping pretty hard over there. You sure ya'll weren't smoking together?" she said nastily.

"Yeah, bitch. Me, him, and your grandmother smoke up before she sucks our dicks, bitch," I yelled back to her, just as nastily. Another cop blindsided me in the ribs and I felt my breath escape me.

I was slammed back into the chair, hitting my head on the wall in the process. The safe was carried back into the place. It had somehow been blasted open with God only knows what. The cops' greedy eyes lit up when they saw the stacks of money.

"Well, looky here. Nine thousand dollars," someone said, which was a blessing in disguise because anything over ten was another charge from the IRS. I looked back into my kitchen and saw more cops digging in the closet where I kept the .380, and I knew they would find it shortly. I just sat back and counted down to myself. 1 . . . 2. . . .

"Hey, what's this?" one called out. "Look what we found!" said the other. He spun the gun around on his finger. A law had just been passed in Maryland that any illegal handgun was an automatic five years, no parole. My bones began to shake as the weed and the gun assured me two very bad felonies. I knew I was going to jail for a very long time.

"So, Mr. Wise. You still wanna play big-shot bravado? Or are you gonna do the smart thing and come forward?" the old white dude tried again.

"Man, take me to prison! A rat? Apparently, you never heard what the late, great John Gotti said: 'Under no circumstances do you tell. You catch a beef, you take your rap.' I'm not telling shit," I told him. I was hit in the ribs once more by some dude who looked like Jesse Ventura. The pain couldn't be diminished, but it had felt good to stand up to the cops. I was proud of myself. I assured my realness to myself and to my friends. My loyalty to my friends could never be challenged again.

I started wracking my mind, thinking about who the rat could be. My cell phone rang and one of the cops picked it up and put it on speakerphone.

"Hey, man, don't come over here. That party over," he said to my caller.

"Who dis?" they asked.

"The police," and the line quickly went dead while the room of cops roared with laughter. Whoever it had been must've gotten the picture and hung up. I couldn't believe this was happening. They had me dead in the water. Twelve pounds of weed and an illegal semiautomatic handgun. Not to mention the nine thousand five hundred dollars in cold cash. I was caught red handed and I had no defense. I would have to cop out to whatever they offered. My shock at all this prevented an outburst, but I knew that sooner or later, it would hit me and crush my world. I was so relieved that it wasn't about the murder that I actually smiled. The police ransacked my place and didn't find anything else worth their time. They took my keys and searched my car too but came up empty there.

"Call the wagon and get this punk outta here," Harvey ordered a cop.

"Your son's going to social services and his mother can pick him up from there," the white bitch cop told me.

Harvey seemed to show a little compassion and said to me, "I'll tell you what. If his mother can get here to pick him up before the wagon, she can take him tonight. If not, you will probably be charged with child abuse on top of all this." I told him the phone number of Daniel's mother, and he dialed it and put the phone against my ear so I could talk.

"Hey, look. Come get the baby right this minute!" I told her. "I'm in big trouble with the law. I live in 5015 Goodnow. Hurry!" I said and nodded to Harvey who hung up the phone.

She must have sensed the panic in my voice, for my son's mother was there in fifteen minutes flat. My son was still sleeping and had yet to wake up to see what was going on. I heard my son's mother downstairs being greeted by a cop, and I asked to be taken out of sight of her to avoid her verbal tirade that was sure to come. The cop agreed and led me into the bathroom. I heard her calling out to me saying that I was a bitch, among other things. She basically had to be dragged out of my place with her sister holding Daniel. I could hear my son crying from being interrupted in his sleep and it broke my heart. Tears escaped my eyes before I could clamp them shut. I wanted to crawl in a hole and die.

After the police threatened to take her to jail as well, she finally left. Driving off, she could still be heard questioning my manhood out the window. Minutes later the paddy wagon arrived and I was led down the stairs very carefully. If my hands had been free or if it had been at all possible to free my hands, I would've grabbed a cop's pistol and put two in my head for my stupidity. Why the hell had I been lounging around with all that weed? I had broken hustling's number one rule: Never keep your drugs where you lay your head.

I was thrown into the back of the wagon by the same short bald due from before. The door slammed shut and I was hauled off to jail.

Chapter 21

The shock at the unexpected raid was beginning to wear off as I sat in the dingy holding cell. A correctional officer came by as I was processed and slid my charging papers under the steel door for me to read.

Count 1. Possession with the intent to distribute marijuana.

Count 2. Possession of a firearm while in the possession of a controlled substance.

Count 3. Possession of paraphernalia.

Count 4. Possession of a controlled substance.

Combined, the maximum sentence would be twenty-six years. The first two counts were felony charges and carried the bulk of the twenty-six. I kind of felt relieved that it was finally over. The ripping, the running, the fast exchange of currency, the sneakiness it took to conceal illegal activity, the reliance on marijuana to fend off the stress of the game. It was finally all over. It felt strange but joyful. A feeling of relief filled my soul when I thought about the opportunity at a new life. I was caught up in the web of hustling drugs and I knew I had finally been untangled. No matter the consequences, it all seemed worth it.

My only regret was that one of my friends had done such an evil thing against me. Who could it possibly be? Toni? Steve? Fats? Of course not any of them. I really had no idea. It could have been anyone. I read the charge papers again, this time the summary of the case. It said that the police had received a tip from an unknown source and that the person refused to reveal their identity in fear of retaliation. It was also noted that I was not under investigation and that someone had done the police a favor. But who? I hadn't the slightest idea, and chances were that I never would. The thought of not being able to give Steve's mother the lawyer money upset me. The money was basically flushed down the toilet when it could have gone to a good cause. I never even considered the police raiding my home.

This wasn't supposed to be; it wasn't in my script. They had caught me sleeping with twelve pounds of weed. I deeply regretted my decision not to answer sales for two days. I was pretty sure I would have sold well over four pounds by now. What was I thinking? The double drama threw me way off course.

First the fallout with Toni, which should have been avoided. I should have smoked the weed in the comfort of my own home. Her preference should have been overruled by my dominance in my own house. Actually, it had all led up from my procrastination in taking the trip. I should have already left by now. Then Steve. I should have cleared my apartment the second I heard about his arrest. I should have been strong enough to move on. I allowed myself to shut down because of the awful news. I should have listened to my conscience telling me to get the weed away from me. I had somehow the devil to assure me that it was all okay, and it had subsequently led to my downfall.

I sat mesmerized at my train of thought. I suddenly realized what I had been doing wrong. I noticed I kept saying "should have" this and "should have" that. But it was all over and there was no chance to go back and change anything. Everything had happened for a reason, and it was time to take full responsibility for my actions and decision. I knelt down against the filthy concrete and prayed softly.

"Lord, please forgive me for my lewd acts that went against you. I beg for no mercy for I knew full well what I was doing was wrong. I thank you that the murder is not among the charges against me. Amen," I finished and stood up, glancing around the cell. The sight of so many black men caged together was despicable. When will we, as African Americans, ever see the trap? I had a good feeling that I wouldn't be as successful in my plea for a low bail.

The C.O. came and called six of our names to see the commissioner. My stomach filled with anxiety as I walked into the small office separated by thick glass. I sat down in the chair provided and listened to the omnipotent-sounding voice coming down from the speaker. I was informed of the charges against me and told to sign multiple papers concerning my rights. A large sign warmed me against stealing any writing utensils. The short white lady with huge glasses stared at the paper listing my alleged charges. She abruptly stood up and disappeared without excusing herself.

I sat wondering about my fate. Representation of various city drug strips decorated the walls and desk, graffiti that was probably done in the absence of the commissioner. Minutes later, the nerdy-looking lady returned to her chair.

"Mr. Wise, I cannot release you on your own recognizance because the possibility of incarceration is significant. But I do see you have no criminal record, so I will set your bail at fifteen thousand dollars," she told me. I tried to speak but was cut off.

"I'm not a judge, so please save your comments. Thank you, have a nice day. Make sure you leave the pen. Goodbye now," she told me and the door opened by a C.O. who was waiting to escort me to be interviewed by a pre-trial counselor. Only three people at a time were allowed in the cubicle. As we waited patiently, a slip of paper was slid under the door indicating that the interviews taking place were now complete. Two black boys with braids were shoved in along with myself.

One of the dudes, a big light-skinned guy who stood well over six feet five inches tall, spoke out of turn and began cussing the lady out when asked his name.

"Bitch, what the fuck is your name, huh? Ya'll motherfuckers always asking dumbass questions! Fuck Central Booking! Fuck ya'll," he hollered. He banged on the glass, which startled the frail black lady behind it. Three hefty C.O.s answered a call for help, two big dudes and a woman. The thugged-out dude was dragged out and quickly dissipated. Thuds and thumps could be heard over top of the cries for help. The walls shook, indicating that the tall out-of-control dude had been slammed into the concrete.

"Next. What's your name, sir?" The lady was back to business. I guess scenes like that were nothing new around here. After hearing some stranger give the lady all his personal information, I gave mine. He slid the paper under the door, and a guard came answering minutes later.

We were taken to the shower area and forced to strip down naked and bathe around ten men. I felt embarrassed revealing myself around all those men. I had taken privacy for granted, and it seemed to be a luxury at this point. I dick and balled it quickly and stepped out with my hand cupped over my penis. A guard stood at the door and handed out towels. My clothing was gone, replaced with a yellow jumper that resembled a banana. My Timberlands and socks remained intact, and I dressed in the new outfit and was led to a line for the phones.

Three phones were bolted to the wall, but only one of them worked. I became frustrated at the conditions and said aloud, "This is bullshit. How is it that one fuckin' phone work?" I complained. Seeing the six guys in front of me made my blood boil hotter. Would I even get a chance to use the damn phone? I knew that ten percent of my fifteen thousand dollars would have me out in no time. I relaxed and the resources I had access to made me feel like I counted.

With only two guys left in front of me, the large C.O. spoke, "Listen up, gentlemen. The elevator is on its way. Ya'll going upstairs?"

"What about the phone?" I whined.

"That shit dead, homebody," he answered.

The elevator doors opened, and all ten of us were packed inside like sardines. The elevator door didn't close until a C.O. stepped into the cramped booth. He held a badge up to the camera in the left-hand corner and the door shut immediately. We were herded to the fifth floor and a small dark-skinned woman was awaiting our arrival. After checking our armbands, she assigned cell numbers.

"Donny Wise, bed number 48, top bunk," and after the ten of us were assigned, she opened a door that led to a large room with six rounded tables. Stools bolted to the floors surrounded the tables and the two TVs that provided an aerial view. Fifteen pitiful-looking faces in yellow suits stood around staring at us, trying to identify familiar faces. It seemed as though everyone knew somebody except me, probably because I was raised in the county as opposed to the city. No one acknowledged me or even spoke, and I sat alone on the round steel table. I saw an opening for the phone and made a dash for it.

I had been under arrest for nearly twenty-four hours, and this was my first chance at a phone call.

"Yo, my man. My buddy was next," some guy yelled but I continued dialing the number. I was angry, frustrated, and tired. I was in no mood for catering to assholes or their favoritism.

"I know," I said sarcastically, remembering these two guys making multiple calls earlier. "I'll only be a minute," I said. On the third ring, I heard my brother answer like he was anticipating my call. The operator began her introduction and warning against three-way calls and just as she finished her speech, the phone hung up. What the fuck? I turned around in shock only to see the brown guy hollering about him being next.

"You were just on the muthafucka!" I yelled in his face. They were fucking with me because I was light-skinned, and they figured I was some pretty boy who was too scared to stand up for myself. Before I completed my thought, though, I had thrown two fierce right hooks followed by an uppercut. The hooks were blocked, but my uppercut landed neatly. The frail man staggered a little before charging me, and I grabbed a mesh of his nappy hair and slung him into the wall. I kneed his stomach with my thigh before slamming him on his face. I gripped his hair for dear life until it became dislodged and fell into my hand. I kicked the guy until blood ran from his nose and mouth simultaneously. The guard had seen the brawl, but because of her small stature, she chose to turn her back.

Some old man pulled me off the guy; my fresh Timberlands saturated in blood. He pulled me into the shower and turned on the water. I was about to attack this old man until he urgently told me to wash the blood off my hands and boots.

"Calm down, young fella," he said soothingly to me. My breathing was frantic, and tears of anger and frustration clouded my vision.

"Man, I want to go home, Pops. And that was my chance and that bitch hung up on my peoples!" I complained, tears streaming down my face.

"I know, I know. Them fuckers been doing that to everybody. But he won't mess with you no more," the old man assured me.

After cleaning me up, we returned to the large room. Five C.O.s were questioning people about what had happened. They looked at me and knew that I was somehow involved. My boots were soaked and I still had a demonic look on my face. Everyone, including the victim of my rage, said that nothing happened, and they locked down the tier in attempt to persuade the victim to come forward.

"What cell you in?" the old man asked me.

"48."

"Good, come on. You wit' me," he told me and we walked in. I climbed up on my bunk and pictured taking my frustrations out on the skinny punk.

"He deserved it, son. Guess what he did to me?" and then the old man began telling me how the kid hung up on his wife then hogged the phone until lock-in time. The man must have been in his seventies. I couldn't help but as why he was in jail in the first place.

"I got caught drinking and driving and they searched my car and found a little 'ready rock.' I smoke it every now and then," he confessed. *Damn*, I thought. A seventy-year-old coke smoker. What was the world coming to?

"How old are ya, man?" I asked him.

"I'm fifty-nine. Just turned fifty-nine yesterday, in fact. Yep, locked up on my birthday, on my way home from the bar to fuck my old lady. Had just took a little Viagra and everything. I was going to tear her ass up!" he laughed at his own joke, revealing a deteriorated set of teeth.

"Well, I'm here because my friend dropped a dime on me, ain't that fucked up?" I said, convinced it was severely fucked up.

"Yup," he answered, uninterested. He pulled out a half-piece cigarette that he had somehow managed to smuggle in. He retrieved an old matchbook from his raggedy old dress shoes. "You'd be surprised what an old man like me can get away with," he said as though he had read my thoughts. "You smoke?" he asked.

"Not cigarettes. But as bad as my nerves are, I am today," I told him and glanced at the cigarette. He lit it quickly and took two hard pulls before passing it to me. I hit it with caution, wondering if he had hidden it in his ass. The nicotine made my head spin like a Ferris wheel and I gave it back to him.

"I'm done," I told him and he continued smoking until the filter was burning. Then he flushed it. I lay back, my head spinning and knuckles throbbing, and closed my eyes and eventually dozed off.

Chapter 22

I woke up at the crack of dawn to what I thought were hands all over me. Only what I thought were hands turned out to be small roaches crawling all over my body. I slapped myself in the places I felt the intruders crawling and heard a crunch and felt their tiny footsteps scatter for cover. I felt a sticky goo on my stomach, which I attributed to roach guts, and I used my make-shift sheet to wipe myself clean, but I still felt like the insects were crawling all over me. It was psychological at this point; the sight of the roaches had sent me over the edge, shockwaves reverberating throughout my body. I got up and rinsed myself off as best as I could and then I noticed what had drawn the insects to me in the first place. A moldy piece of lunchmeat was stored underneath my bunk. Someone must have forgotten about it, let it there by accident, or left it there as a sick joke, knowing it would bring roaches out from everywhere.

I paced about my cell with the old man sleeping peacefully, and I began doing pushups, hoping to shake my jitters. At fourteen, my arms nearly collapsed. It had been well over three years since the last time I had tried calisthenics, and my body was badly out of shape. The only exercise I got daily was from fucking aggressive bitches, battling over positions and using my muscles only to dominate them and for nothing else. Other than that, lifting the blunt forty-five degrees was the only times my arms got any action.

I was reluctant to lie back on my roach-infested mattress, so I just walked around the tiny cell. The possibility of being home by now made me wanna beat on that son of a bitch even more. The steel toilet leaded a strong stench of misfired urine. Traces of vomit could be seen stuck to the walls. This was the worst living condition I had ever seen in my life. And to top it off, a small rodent's reflection could be seen patrolling the bottom of the door. He probably smells the meat, I thought, picturing the small mouse dancing on my chest while I slept.

I flushed the meat down the toilet, and the noise made the old man wake up temporarily and mutter, "Martha, come lay yo ass down!" and then he rolled over and went back to sleep. The old man had called me his wife, I thought bizarrely to myself. This couldn't get any worse. I cautiously climbed back on my bunk, using my bag of street clothes for a pillow.

I tossed and turned until morning feed up; the electronic door opened and a working man threw us two brown bags and two tiny cartons of low-fat milk. Inside the bags were two boiled eggs, a cup of cornflakes with three sugar packets, and four pieces of bread with sample packets of jelly matted into a cellophane wrapper. A finicky eater, I gave my boiled eggs and milk to the old man. I poured the sugar into the dry cup of cereal and sprinkled it into my mouth like it was a beverage. I smeared a bit of jelly on each piece of cold bread and folded it in half, using my spoon as a knife.

"You don't put milk in your cereal?" my cell buddy asked as he wolfed his breakfast down.

"Pops, uptown I don't eat cereal," I said, trying to sound like a big shot. "And I can't stand the smell and aftertaste of eggs." I continued eating the lousy breakfast as if it were my last meal. I drank down some lukewarm water to wash down my dry bread. The water tasted like rusted metal that lacked filtration and purity.

I jumped back on my bunk and spotted the dead roach from my wee hour assault; plucked him off my bed and flung him on the floor. It almost landed on the old man's grayish hair, which made me laugh softly. I lay down, fully dressed, on my bunk and stared at the ceiling. Lord knows I needed and had begged for a change, but I never imagined this was what my change would be. I had learned a valuable lesson: never ask God to change something that you can change yourself. I had no idea that this was the change I had been praying for. But I guess he did answer my prayers, for I wasn't slinging weed anymore, now was I?

I dreaded the revenge from the phone   check boys, but I instantly downplayed it. What the hell? If they did get me, I would get those bitches one by one. I knew I was at a complete disadvantage because of my cell buddy. If something kicked off, I couldn't rely on him to thump with me. He would probably fuck around and have a stroke, I joked to myself. I tried to close my eyes, but the vivid reality that my life had been completely turned upside down haunted me greatly. This was only the beginning. I still had to hire counsel, find a new apartment, find a new hustle, and there was still the chance of being associated with those horrible murders. It was beginning to mount on me. The weight on my shoulders made me feel like I couldn't even stand up straight.

I thought about how good I had it not even forty-eight hours ago. The freedom to roam the earth as I wished, a clean record, money, prestige. Why had I taken it all for granted? I had already realized that selling weed couldn't produce a retirement check, let alone a stable income for the family I yearned for. I had been employed at several different organizations, but I always chose to leave them for the lure of fast money. Face it, making a thousand dollars a day had trapped me mentally. I had become too complacent in a lifestyle that changes in the flash of an eye, and now I was paying its exorbitant price. Now none of it seemed worth the consequences I was soon to face. I was so glad that I had given Steve the five thousand dollars and had paid all my monthly expenses. That alone totaled over eight thousand dollars, and the D's almost recovering eighteen thousand dollars in money and smoke nearly broke my back. I refused to add up the total financial ruin I was facing, not only in face value but the heavy aftermath that was due to come from this.

The depression began mounting, and my mind was as anguished as a forty-year-old man's was. Instead of enjoying life with the exuberance and vibrancy of a twenty-one-year-old man, I was suffering severe stress and anxiety from the rotten game of the underworld. The cutthroats, the crooked cops, the customers trying to get over, violence, weighing and packing, the fake friends. The snitchers and haters outnumbered the real niggas and gangstas. I had been the victim of some asshole's jealousy, for my Flash Gordon characteristics were envied by someone who hung close enough to gather information and then have me infiltrated.

The smell of feces snapped me out of my deep thoughts. Pops was taking a shit and the smell was so powerful I had to hold my nose.

"Damn, Pop. Put some cut on that, God damn!" I said to him and he flushed the toilet but continued to defecate. My nostrils were temporarily relieved from the rancid smell of Pop's waste.

Goodness gracious! There were so many aspects of free life that I had taken for granted. So many small things. I noticed the old man wiping his ass with a brown paper bag. Someone had pissed on the toilet paper and left it to dry.

I turned my head away from him to assure that he wouldn't get the wrong idea. I burst out into laughter to prevent from breaking down. This was a rough camp and it was only the beginning.

* * *

Hours that seemed like days passed before they finally opened the doors to allow us out to make our phone calls. Seven of the fifteen faces had departed sometime in the night. A white boy was dialing a number when I walked up on him. He glanced behind me and saw me standing there, patiently waiting for the phone and hung up quickly.

"Just making sure it worked," he mumbled like a scared old woman.

"Man, make your phone call. I'm just next, that's all," I reassured him. I had no intention of becoming the holding tier bully, but he insisted, so I played into the role.

"Stand right here and watch my back. Anyone get within ten feet, you tap me on the shoulder," I ordered him.

"Yessir," he responded and took his post while I made my call to my brother's house. He wasn't home and I started to panic. Where the hell was he? I tried my mother's phone but remembered that she was at work. The only contact number I had for half the people I knew were cell phone numbers, which were prohibited on jail collect phones. I called Matthew, hoping he would answer, and was delighted when I heard a faint, "Hello."

I waited for the operator to finish speaking until I said, "Yo, what's up, son? Somebody snitched, son. . . . Yeah, I'm at Central Booking. I need fifteen thousand dollars. . . . Hold on," I was interrupted by a tap on my shoulder. I turned around and saw a homosexual standing within ten feet; he was trying to make eye contact with anyone who liked boys, I guessed. Fuck him. I turned my attention back to the phone.

"Hey, Matt, can you spring me, my man? . . . Thank you . . . I'll pay you back. . . . Okay, how long? . . . Thanks yo, I love you," I told him and I hung up the phone with joy.

At least I wouldn't have to spend another night in prison. I knew nothing about bail bondsmen, but I figured it would take about ten hours before everything was finalized and I was released.

I turned around and, to my surprise, I didn't see the dude whose face I had beaten to a pulp last night but a small clique of chumps were mugging me when convenient. I threw my head up and popped my collar twice, indicating my lack of concern. I was showing my ass because I knew I was going home in a matter of hours. I prayed that Matt would jump on the task at hand. I was comfortable that he would because we had been friends for nearly fifteen years . . . since Pop Warner football we had been running together. I even called his mother "Ma" occasionally, even though she was white.

Steve and I had become close since doing capers in the mid-nineties, which wasn't Matt's style. He was the Honest Abe of the crew and, next to Braino, had the most money. He had been stacking trap money for six years straight, only being jammed one time with an eighth of a brick for which he received three years' probation. (Because of his color, was my personal opinion.)

I sat down at the half full steel table and listened to some white man explain how he had been arrested for Ecstasy in East Baltimore. The man was every bit of sixty. It reminded me of Pops, an old-time hustler who used his SSI to flip weed money.

I felt a pair of eyes burning a hole into the back of my head and glanced up to see that faggy was staring me down. I turned my head and put up my middle finger, as if scratching my temple, although it was obvious I was giving him the bird. I glanced back at him and shook my head with my mug broke. I was in no mood to allow some masculine sissy to bust off to my physique. I was absolutely startled to see some big black guy rapping with the punk. I watched as they disappeared in the back with caution. Maybe he wasn't staring at me after all, I decided.

At any rate, the thought made me cringe. Pops came and tapped me on the shoulder.

"Hey young'un. You talk to your folks?"

"Yeah. You getting out?" I asked him.

"Yeah, I just talked to my wife. She tired. Tired of going through my bullshit. That woman done bailed me out more times than years we been married. My bail only one thousand dollars. I need a hundred dollars and she talk' 'bout I might have to sit until court. Ain't that some shit? Man, I'm a kick her fat ass when I do get out," he declared.

"Then you'll be right back here," I jokingly reminded him.

"Well, fuck it. Already out on two or three bails, what's one more?" he said. I felt like kicking his old ass. How ignorant he sounded! Out on three bails and mad at the poor lady who was just tired of spending all her money. If he wasn't my cell buddy, I would have told him how fucked up he was. Instead I turned my back to him and finished listening to the white man exaggerate.

An hour went past and six more black dudes in banana suits were escorted in. *More blacks caught up in the web*, I thought. I mentally tallied the ratio of guys. Out of twenty-five guys, twenty-two of us were black, the other three were white. That made roughly 80 percent African-American, not to mention the seven guys who had already left were black, too. I shook my head, ashamed, for I knew so much better. I had taken courses at Coppin State College on black history, and I was alarmed at the statistics. I had no business being in a confined place with so many black people. I was smarter than this, at least that's what I thought. I vowed to make a difference in society and not just be another statistic, but I knew money was also a statistic. It was all a game of numbers. I sat there, deep in my thoughts and in a somber mood.

Everything was so clear. Why was it so hard to see such blatant obviousness? Every hood in America knew about the rumors of the government allowing drugs in the city and county, leading to direct distribution from the black man. So why did we all fall for the trap and continue to eat from the poisonous cheese that was dangled in front of us?

I withdrew the piece of pencil I had clipped from the pre-trail counselor and went to the closest wall out of sight of the C.O. and wrote:

Wake up Black Man! Jail is a trap! Drugs are the cheese
and we are the rats! Houses, cars, clothes, trips, jewelry, and
money are supposed to be our goals. Instead it's agony,
death, or incarceration before we're thirty years old. Killing
each other over petty drug turf, snatchin' purses to feed
that craving habit. Snitchin' on your fellas for immunity.
Too many thugs, dope fiends, and snakes that live in our
community. Those of us that do make it to jail see far
too many familiar faces. Overcrowded prisons, 88%
black faces, that should tell you who's losing these
races. It's set up like an extinction project, eliminate
those most feared. So they provide us with drugs and
give us life sentences so eventually we turn queer. They
know the black man loves to have sex, stickin' his black
penis to soothe sexual taste. Weaker men are sacrificed,
turned into prison bitches, made to wear lipstick and dye
their hair with liquid base. Still we continue to get higher
for drugs are snuck through the door. Crooked C.O.s look
the other way, for the right price, when drugs are brought
to their floor.

Does it get any clearer, my brotha?
Would your situation be different if you were any other color?
Yes! Well let's stop sleeping and wake up and reduce the
Numbers under white covers.

When I finished writing my reality poem, I turned around, only to see a small crowd of inmates watching every word as I wrote it. One short brown-skinned guy shook my hand.

"My brova. I can't read that good but it's a beautiful poem," he said to me.

"Thank you. Would you like me to read it to you?" I offered.

"Yes, yes, please." And so I did.

Chapter 23

After twelve hours of pacing, wondering, and a lengthy nap, I was finally released. I stood on the corner, watching the car turn onto Route 83. It dawned on me how late it was by the sparse traffic out this beautiful night. I had no money in my pockets or in my house. I didn't have the nerve to call Matt and beg for a ride after he put up the 10 percent.

I walked to a nearby Chinese joint and called my mother collect. She answered the call and agreed to come get me.

"I'm standing right in front of the jail, Ma." I hung up and thought about the luxury of the Chinese food I smelled. Everything seemed like a privilege. Walking back across the street to my original location, my mother pulled up in her old Volvo 240.

I jumped in the car and was given a huge bear hug. My mother was crying softly as church music blared through her speakers.

"Give you life to Christ, Donny," she begged, still holding on to me tightly until three cars beeped loudly behind her.

She shifted into drive and made the sharp right turn onto 83. She was heading toward her house until I reminded her that I needed my car.

"Oh, that's right," she said and detoured on Cold Spring East and headed toward Monrovia. For the first time, I really took her plea to seek religion seriously. I had a personal relationship with God, but on my own terms. I didn't openly repent to God until I was in trouble, and then I would whine, *Why why why?* I saw myself now as being selfish, listening to the young woman on the radio sing about salvation. Just like everything else, religion is a two-way street. You can't only drink from the well; you must also bring water when you come.

"Shoving God above your true love will free and cleanse your soul like a dove. . . ." the woman sang out on the radio.

I really began giving my mother's words a lot of thought and consideration. When we pulled up, I asked my mother to wait a couple minutes. I didn't know what to expect.

I entered the lobby and, anticipating a ransacked sight, darted up the three flights of steps to my floor. My door was basically glued back together and my doorknob was attached loosely. I basically tapped on the door and it swung open, and a huge lump formed in my throat.

My place was fucking empty. I almost passed out as tears shot from my eyes like a faucet. My TV was gone, my clothes, even my fuckin' underwear. My shoes. The place was wiped clean. I never had a full house of furniture, for it had only been five weeks since I had my apartment. I opened my fridge and even my half gallon of OJ had disappeared. I had well over ten thousand dollars worth of outfits missing from their hangers. My collection of seven Coogi sweaters was gone. My Avirex leather jackets swiped. My Gucci loafers, Air Max, Timberlands—*adios. Everything.* Anything of value I had had been clipped.

I felt like I couldn't breathe; I really felt the sails in my lungs collapse.

"Jesus, no! Please save me!" I called out and punched a hole in the wall. I had blood in my mouth and murder on my mind. Even the dining room set I had just had delivered a week before the raid had been stolen. Somebody or something had basically backed a truck against the door and wiped my ass clean. As an insult, my safe lie in the middle of the floor, a gaping hole where the door had once been.

I was snapped out of my misery by the sound of horns blaring from outside. I had forgotten all about my mother. With nothing of value left in the house, I grabbed a stack of important investment papers and left the door wide open. I reached into my pocket to feel my car keys for the fifth time. I couldn't believe what had happened to my apartment. I was in total shock and disbelief.

The fuckin' cops might as well have put a sign on my door announcing a neighborhood yard sale. The repair to my door was so shitty that it had probably been pried open with a baseball card. And the worst part about the whole ordeal was nobody would take responsibility for replacing my belongings. I had been fucked on all four corners.

I walked out of the lobby, pale as a ghost, like I had seen the devil himself. My mother, agitated by my long "coupla minutes," begged for an explanation. I tried to hold back my tears, for I knew once it rained it would pour.

"What happen?" she asked, concern all over her face.

"Ma, somebody robbed my apartment and stole all my stuff," I told her, and the reality rang throught my body and the tears broke their dam. I cried so hard I felt like I couldn't breathe. My extravagant wardrobe had boosted my self-esteem. Over sixty pairs of shoes made me walk with a strut. Now with only the one pair of boots I had on, I felt flat-footed. My swagger was gone, my confidence shot. I had gone from riches to rags overnight.

117

I collapsed into my mother's loving arms. I was crushed. This chain of events had simply engulfed my will to fight. I was ready to throw the white flag in and surrender.

My mother, in disbelief after I got the whole story out coherently, ran up the stairs to my former apartment. I heard a shrill scream, and I knew she had seen the apartment. She came back down with a yellow paper in her hand.

"I know you don't wanna see this. But this was on the inside of the door," and she thrust it at me. I took the eviction notice and read it. It said I breached my lease by having illegal drugs in my residence, which by law gave them the right to evict me in ten days. My signature at the bottom of the lease acknowledged this, they were quick to remind me, and provided me with a copy of my lease.

I balled it up in my fist. "Those mothe—" but I stopped myself when I remembered my mother was there. "The freakin' maintenance men probably the ones who brought the U-Haul." Before tossing the trash on the ground, I peed at the lengthy fine of six hundred dollars they were trying to stick me with for the inconvenience and the embarrassment to the neighborhood.

"I know a man you can rent a room from if you don't wanna stay with me. He only charges forty dollars a week," my mother told me. I was listening to the soft gospel music in the car.

Fuck that, I'm goin' to get high, I wanted to say, but I didn't. I only thought it. Thought it hard. I clutched my car keys in my hand, my eyes a deep red from crying hysterically for the past fifteen minutes.

"Ma, I gotta go get some smoke. I'll holla at you later tonight or tomorrow."

"Okay, son. Be careful and I love you. Here—gimme a hug, Donny," she said and I hugged her hard and got out of her car and into mine. I started the ignition and revved her up. I had totally forgotten about my man Stevey, and I hoped and prayed he was all right.

I knew the word would spread about my arrest, and I knew he didn't think I would put his people on front street with the lawyer money. Only death or incarceration stopped me from looking out for my people.

Besides, Steve was in jail because of me. I had lost the precious dope, and that made the white boys buck. I had to show some love. I considered writing my old dog Glenn, who was doing life in prison, to see if I could purchase a contract on the brothers, but the soft tunes of the gospel music I had listened to in Ma's car came flooding into my mind and I reconsidered. Not to mention, I had to succumb to meager living and I no longer had the funds available for shit like that. Yeah, I could always get jump started or fronted, but the fact that a wolf lay among us was too risky. The bastard might have been my favorite customer for all I knew. I didn't know and didn't wanna find out, for it would force me to draw blood and I would certainty go to prison for the rest of my life. It just wasn't worth it, but I *was* curious.

A burning desire to make the man—or woman—suffer ate at me. If I was able to identify, I would be sure to have the fur tore off their ass within twenty-four hours. I wasn't a killer, but I ran with killers. I drove on, listening to Marvin Gaye.

I needed weed, and with a full tank of gas, I did what any other fiend would have done—I hacked.

I saw someone flagging their hand and made a U-turn; they couldn't believe that a luxury car was in the business. That made two of us, I chuckled. The dude with dreadlocks jumped in the back.

"Naw, yo, sit in the front," I told him because I wanted to reduce my chances of being robbed by him, shot in the back of the head, or flapped (when the customer jumps out without paying). He obliged and gave me his destination when he got in the passenger seat. It just so happened that he was going to a weed spot.

"Take me to Carey and Lanvale. I hope them batman are still out," he said, looking at his watch. "Plus, yo, I want to come back to my girl house, so I want you to wait," he ordered me. This Rasta must have mistaken me for a dope fiend, so I had to clear the air quick.

"Yo, give me ten dollars for the round trip, but just cop me a bag of weed and get me a Dutch."

"All right. Bet," he smiled at me and I saw that his teeth had gold fronts with initials on them.

The strip was still jumping when we pulled up and I parked the car a little ways down the street. He got out, leaving his pager behind on accident. I laughed, thinking he could go ahead and stiff me now if he wanted to, looking at the expensive two-way.

Minutes later, he came back with four pregnant turkeys. The weed bags were so stuffed they had to be stapled shut. As he was getting back in the car, he noticed his mistake.

"Oh, shit, my box!" and then looked at me and I just looked back at him with an honest look on my face. He looked surprised and said, "Yo, that's some cool shit. Hold on another minute," and he dashed back to the corner. He came back not even a minute later with the Dutches and another pillow sack.

"Yo, take two bags for not peeling with my beeper." He gave me two pregnant bags and three Dutches, and I thought, *Damn, hacking ain't so bad after all.* To complete his generosity, he rolled up a cannon on the way back to North Avenue, where I had I picked him up. My mouth watered with anticipation; it had been a year ago that I had gone three days without smoking a blunt. I was definitely addicted and I didn't care.

He lit it up and passed it to me, and I hit it hard and strong, doing multiple tricks with the smoke to flaunt my professionalism with the herb. When we got back to North and Eutaw, dude put the blunt out and got out the car. He held his hand out and gave me five dollars.

"Man, I paid two hundred for this joint earlier today and I can't believe I almost lost it. Good lookin' out. Take care," he said and threw the money in the seat and took off down the street.

"Done!" I yelled after him and pulled off. Three days ago, that chump would have been working for me. Now he was hooking me up and giving me chicken box money.

I stopped at the all-night chicken joint and ordered two boxes of chicken. The total came to $5.80 and all I had was the $5 dude had given me. I was so embarrassed that I told them that I changed my mind and wanted the ten wings and a half-n-half. It left me with $0.17 in my pocket.

I drove back to my mother's house and went inside. I flashed the smoke and the grub at her.

"You aight wit' me son, now roll dat up." And we both laughed and we both rolled our own Dutch out of only one dimebag. I was used to rolling blunts outta pounds, and now here I was, pinching it out of the tiny dime bag.

"Jeezy, weezy. Life is a rough camp, all right," I said, shaking my head.

We ate the chicken first, then went to my favorite spot to smoke—the roof. We pulled out lawn chairs and smoke our blunts, looking out at the stars. The reefer was powerful and my mother choked her head off.

"I see why they call it 'action hero' now," she said in between coughs. We sat there smoking silently and finally relaxed enough to kick my feet up. Life wasn't that bad, looking through my glassy eyes. Everything seemed so peaceful. Me and my mother—who would have ever though that moments earlier, I was contemplating doing a swan dive off the very roof we were smoking on.

The stress of the game, the consequences, everything. I had only been exposed to the glamorous side of the game. Now it was like the grim reaper was creeping up on me, forcing me to see the ugly side of things. Gone was the sunlight and happiness of my life, and it was like a whole 'nother world.

My mother left me when she saw I had stopped answering her questions. I was in deep thought and she knew my moods. When I finally returned to earth, I noticed that I was on the roof alone and I didn't feel like moving just yet.

So I said fuck it and kicked off my shoes. I stretched back on the chair and spent the night on the roof.

Chapter 24

Birds were chirping and the sun was shining bright when I finally woke and came to my senses. I had forgotten I was on the roof until I saw a telephone pole that was lying horizontally and—what the fuck—realized I was lying on top of the roof. I laughed at myself for actually spending a full night outside. I always knew I was a natural savage.

I carefully climbed back in the window with my boots in my hand. It was 9:19 A.M. and my mother had already left for work. I wondered why she didn't come get me from the roof before she left.

I skipped down the steps, hearing the TV on, and to my surprise I saw my brother passed out on the couch, full dressed. I must have woken him up because he squirmed left and right before groggily opening his eyes.

"Where the hell you been, stranger?" he asked me, sitting up.

"On the roof," I joked, and we embraced each other.

"Mommy called me and told me 'bout what happen; she told me everything. Don't worry, you know what will happen if that hater is identified," he reassured me. "I talked to the man you supposed to be renting the room from; he wants to meet you," he finished.

I went to the kitchen sink to wash my face and try to clear the cobwebs in my mind. I felt like a sleepwalking robot.

"Here, spark this," Rock suggested and handed me a Caribbean Round; it must have contained a quarter ounce in it.

"But yo, I thought we was goin' to see the landlord." I didn't want to be all high and stupid in front of my prospective landlord.

Rock laughed, "Nigga, he smoke." So oh well, I hit the zooka and we walked out the front door, my eyes searching for his humongous truck. Instead I followed him to a long Crown Victoria with pipes, and it couldn't have been newer than 1988.

"Soon's I found out you been told on, I went and copped a hoop-dog. Put the Expo on ice for a month, ya feel me?" He explained his choice in wheels as we got inside.

"Yeah, smart move, man," I agreed.

The interior of the car, however, wasn't as raggedy as the outside. It had been equipped with a flip-out DVD/navigation system. The joint was cozy and the ride smooth.

I coughed up some phlegm and spit it on the road while inhaling the intense 'dro. We pulled up at an old dirty house on West Twenty-ninth Street. The man, a young-looking old 'head who thought he was slick, sat on the front steps smoking a joint. He had on jeans, a sweater, and Chess shoes, and he wore his Kangol cap slightly tipped to the left.

I firmly shook his hand, with just a hint of aggressiveness to show him that I was a strong-minded man, and he led me upstairs to the back room that was for rent.

The quarters were already furnished with a twin bed, a small dresser, and an aerial view of Druid Hill Park. The room was built and furnished for a fourteen-year-old boy, but it was better than living at home with my mother, so I decided to go ahead and take it.

My brother got a wad of cash from his pocket and paid my rent up to two months in advance. The guy handed me a key and told me to call him Show Daddy, and I thought, *What a true fucking pimp.* As we left the small house, I began to feel a little better. I could easily hustle up a TV and some clothes.

My brother popped the trunk of his big-ass car and removed four bags and two boxes. "Here. Your first housewarming gift." And he handed me a few bags and we made our way inside with them. I peeked in one of the bags and saw jeans, T-shirts, boxers, and socks. The shoeboxes were a new pair of hiker boots and fresh pair of Air Force Ones. I was thoroughly touched, for his deed was so unexpected and so unlike him. I felt blessed to have such a loving brother.

We carried the bags up to my little room and Rock said, "I suggest you stay here for a month or so and let the heat die. Then you can be my lieutenant on the strip." He offered me a good job, but I was finished with that.

"Nigga, I'm done. The only thing I'm touching is a blunt. I'd rather go get a job for real," I told him honestly. I knew I would lose the few possessions that I was clinging to if I didn't find a good job making good money, and that seemed very impossible with the two felonies hanging over my head.

"Aight, nigga, but minimum wage won't pay for no Acura," Rock said coldly. But then he said, "Come on, I'll drive you back to your car and you can follow me back home." As we were leaving the place, I peeped out the kitchen. It was missing a stove, a refrigerator, and the rusty faucet was leaking. The back door had been nailed shut and the thermostat had been ripped out. My fears were confirmed when I opened the door to the mildew-infested basement and neither saw nor heard a furnace of any kind. My mood plummeted. I was living in a house with no heat or means to store or cook food. I think it was then that it dawned on me that I was a struggling motherfucker.

I met my brother at the car and we rode on in silence. I didn't want to stay with my brother, for I didn't want to invade his privacy, same with my mother, but the living conditions of the house I had just rented seemed a bit extreme. I thought about this decision, whether to stay in the shithole or with one of my peoples. I finally decided to give it a week, if for nothing else, to experience the rough living conditions and just to see if I could do it.

We pulled up next to my car and I jumped in and followed his lead. My brother had an absolutely beautiful apartment. Red Italian leather couches with a red marble coffee table and giant fish tank with two aggressive piranhas with terrified feeder fish swimming around in fear. Deep red and gold Aubusson carpets lined the floors. He had this beautiful ebony curio cabinet, displaying all the monies of the all the foreign countries he had been to. Two Baccarat crystal decanters were filled with XO Cognac and four snifters sat on a Chippendale table beside the cabinet. There were large pictures of his son in fourteen-karat gold frames displayed here and there, and the entire scheme was so coordinated and relaxing. It looked like a showroom from a magazine and like he had probably spent thousands and thousands on some fancy interior decorator, but he hadn't. Just goes to show you that good taste ran in the family.

As soon as I got in the apartment, I took my shoes off, as did everyone so as not to ruin his expensive carpets. He picked up a giant remote control with a screen and hit a few buttons and the dark apartment came to life. The lights came on, the stereo blasted, the big screen ninety-inch Pioneer plasma came to life, and even a bulb lit up in the aquarium.

"I'll be damned," I said softly to myself, impressed. He had one of those smart houses that was wired into a remote control. I couldn't help but be envious, because here I was, flat broke and living in a hole while my brother was living it up in a dream pad. He deserved it, though, for he had worked hard and hustled smart. Nobody besides myself, his woman, or our immediate family was allowed in his luxurious apartment. He never kept a bit of drugs within twenty miles of his home, and the pistol he owned was hard to find and easy to get to. I felt ashamed for being envious and started feeling nothing but the utmost respect for my brother.

He had used his brilliance on the street and brute muscle to earn his place in the game and he deserved it more than anyone did. We drank the XO, ate steamed shrimp, and smoked Dutches of purple haze until I finally dozed off, flat on his beautiful Italian leather couch.

* * *

Hard thumps and pants broke my peace. I looked around curiously, confused by the sunlight blazing in the windows. I checked my watch and saw that it was 7:48 A.M. and I had slept for almost fourteen hours. The heavy breathing was coming from the master bedroom; the door was half open and I caught a glimpse of a brown-skinned woman riding my brother. Watching her shadow bounce back and forth, I became aroused. Her breasts were healthy and her hair was long, just the way I liked my women. The haze had thrown me into hibernation and I figured my brother had stepped out and returned with this woman.

Not wishing to disturb him, I gathered myself up and crept out the door. I hopped in my whip, pulled off, and saw the Expedition parked at the end of the block. My agenda was to go job-hunting today. I stopped at the corner and bought a newspaper so I could check the classifieds. I circled every ad I could see for respectable employment with a pen and stopped at the nearest pay phone to call three of them. Federal Express, the post office, and UMMC, who needed a maintenance man. All three confirmed that they were hiring and told me to come immediately to fill out an application.

I rushed home and dick-n-balled it, threw on a fresh outfit from Rock, and swung by Classic Cutz, my favorite barber. Corey tightened my shape up for me, and I was so happy that Rock had thrown me an extra eighty dollars spending money.

I went to the hospital and filled out the application quickly until I came to question number five. "Do you have any arrests, pending or not, for anything other than traffic violations? If yes, please explain." I struggled with what to write down. Would they even give me a chance if I wrote yes? Would they discriminate against me? I decided to fib a little and I circled no, figuring my arrests were early pending and I might be safe.

I left the application and stopped by the post office, where I encountered the same question five, with the exact wording and everything! I circled no, a pro at this, and continued on filling out the rest of the application. I left the post office and drove out to RPS, a division of FedEx, out on Ponca Street.

I felt happy to be doing this one because the money was great and the benefits were excellent. After completing the app, I sat in the waiting room with sixteen other potential employees. They called names alphabetically, so of course I was one of the last to be called. One by one, men came out smiling, full of excitement and pumping their fists in the air. They had all been hired on with a company that took very good care of its employees. So far, ten white guys and five black guys had been added to the roster at FedEx, and I was excited, hoping to be the sixth black guy hired. I finally heard them call "Wise" and I rushed up and flashed the older white lady my best smile as I entered her office and sat down.

She started asking me questions and the interview was going great until she got to question number five.

"So you've never in your life been arrested for anything other than minor traffic violations, Mr. Wise?" she asked me. *It's now or never*, I thought.

"Well, actually I have, but I am convinced that I will prevail in court," I answered, sounding way more confident than I felt.

"What's the charge?" My stomach swelled up and I wanted to die; I could feel my face heating up and sweat dripping down the back of my new shirt. I wanted to lie, but I knew they would do a background check on me anyway.

"Well, they are accusing me of intending to distribute marijuana," I told her honestly.

"Mr. Wise, that's a felony. We don't offer employment to applicants with pending felonies. Good luck somewhere else," she told me, apologetic but not really, and held out her hand. I shook it weakly and gave her a puppy dog look, my heart literally breaking. She wasn't buying it; her tone of voice had changed instantly the minute I was honest with her, and she now looked like she couldn't get me out of her office fast enough. I took a deep breath and just walked out.

I had just known that I was going to get this job and I really wanted it, and the rug had been snatched out from under my feet. Well, I sighed, at least I have the other two jobs I applied for. I was trying to keep faith, but it was dwindling fast.

Both companies were very high profile and prestigious. Forty people might apply for four jobs; the hiring process was competitive and rigorous, I guessed. The smallest flaw would lead to immediate disqualification because there were so many others out there that didn't have a damn thing wrong with their application. I was happy that I had left my mother's phone number as my contact number because she had an answering machine and the call would be picked up.

I went back to Carey and Lanvale and bought a batman and drove home. I was totally frustrated from the way the lady had treated me. The beat-up house didn't even have a phone, let alone a stove to light my blunt, so I stopped at the corner store for a lighter and to call my brother.

"Yo, hey. It's Creamy. I see you was getting your thang this morning. I balled out like 8:00 . . . who was that? . . . WHAT! The pretty bitch from Friday's? . . . Oh shit, yeah I remember that long hair . . . well I just went and put in three apps and I already got shot down by one 'cause of those fuckin felonies. I'll be home. You know the po-lice took my cell and beeper, so come through, holla back." I hung up.

I decided to stay in for the night, so I called up Matt to thank him, ashamed of myself for not having done it the minute I got out.

"Yo, Matty. My bad I ain't holla but them bitches took my cell."

"It's all right," he said.

"Yeah, well I wanted to thank you. I know my brother and mother thanked you, but I been shoulda called. I'm on balls on knuckles right now, but when I get straight, I'm gonna holla," I reassured him.

"Yo, Cream, I love you like a brova, keep the money, yo. I'm about to fuck this scally right quick, so hit me back."

"All right," I said, but he had already hung up. Damn, the soft brushoff approach.

I went into my shithole and rolled the blunt and smoked, staring at the bare walls. My long legs hung off the end of the tiny bed. I lay there, thinking about what to do when the fifty-eight dollars I had left ran out. I wasn't in any shape to keep running to Rock, hacking was too dangerous, and the jobs would take at least three weeks before I drew a paycheck. The unanswered questions sent me into a deep depression. What would I do in two weeks when my four hundred fifty dollar car note and three hundred eighty dollars insurance note was due? I stripped down to my new boxers and smoked until the roach burned my fingers. I then cried myself to sleep, for I had lost everything.

Chapter 25

After two days of hacking and receiving handouts and pulling minor scams, one of the two awaited phone calls finally came. I just happened to be over at my mother's house watching a DVD when the phone rang.

Rushing to answer it, I accidentally kicked over the double deuce of Steel Reserve parked next to my foot.

"Hello?" I answered breathlessly. "This is Donny Wise, yes sir . . . yes sir . . . oh, yes sir. Well, thanks for calling to inform me. . . . You too . . . goodbye." I slammed the phone down. The sons of bitches had done a background check, and therefore, I was immediately eliminated as a prospective employee with the post office. The game was teaching me another grueling lesson. Once you've been labeled a felon, you were blackballed by the rest of society. No employers wanted to hire you, no bank wanted to loan you money, and even colleges shied away from applicants with "felony" attached to their social security number. It all left you with every few choices.

Now I was beginning to see why so many convicted felons continued selling drugs and hustling. They didn't have much choice. My future was bleak and I knew the worst was yet to come. I still had to come up with the four thousand the family attorney wanted to fight the case.

Well, I could only hope and pray that the hospital called me with some good news. With all these steady letdowns and disappointments came the urge to get high. I had started drinking alcohol straight while lying around getting high, blunt after blunt. I even developed the habit of smoking black-n-milds when I couldn't afford weed. It had only been a week and three days since my arrest and I looked ten pounds lighter from my lack of nutrition. I was self-destructing and I couldn't stop it. I had made the terrible mistake of putting all my weight on one foot, so to speak. And when that foot broke from all the pressure, it caused my whole body to collapse. I had relied on selling weed for my whole income. It had paid my credit card bills, phone bills, car note, son's day care, and a host of other responsibilities. Now I was bankrupt with huge debts swimming over my head. I guzzled the remaining 211 Steel Reserve and began laughing; I was drunk from the cheap beer, but that didn't stop my pain from being rejected.

I laughed until I cried. I was starving, but I only had twenty-three dollars left and an empty gas tank. I decided to pull a flam for a coupla bucks.

I grabbed my shirt and headed toward the neighborhood market. The flam was the oldest trick in the book—take twenty-one dollars and buy something that cost two dollars or less. Give the cashier the twenty from your right with the one-dollar bill disguised in your left hand. When she handed me $18.23, my correct change, I swiftly removed the ten from the top and slid the one in on the bottom. I glanced at her strangely.

"Ma'am, may I have my receipt, please?" I looked at the change and quickly slipped the ten in my back pocket.

"Sure, here you go, young man," she gasped, ripping it from the roll. I faked like I was calculating her error when she asked if there was something wrong.

"Yes, you shorted me." I handed her my change and the receipt and she slowly counted $9.23.

"Oh, you know what. I must've given you a one instead of a ten." She took the one-dollar bill from my outstretched hand and replaced it with a ten.

"Sorry 'bout that," she said apologetically and obviously embarrassed.

"That's okay," and I left the market.

I didn't even want the pack of cookies I had used for the front, but I knew I would be hungry later tonight so I stashed them. I got into the car and laughed at myself, recalling the slick move taught to me by a hard-up dope fiend in high school.

I combined the money—twenty dollars. Well, I'd just have to do that a few more times so I could fill up the tank and buy some food. Maybe even a few bags of weed.

I drove around, picking my spots in places that had large crowds. After hitting four more spots throughout the city, I had forty-six dollars and a bunch of junk food. The car, riding on fumes, almost conked out on its way to the gas station. I put sixteen dollars in the tank and bought two batmans and a pint of beef yat mein with extra gravy.

When I got back to my mother's place, I had three dollars left from the scheme, not to mention my original twenty-three dollars.

I rolled a Dutch while checking the answering machine, and to my surprise the hospital had called and left a message saying the pending felonies could have been overlooked for now, but since I had lied on the application, it was an automatic disqualification. I was crushed. I just couldn't win. The black woman's voice on the machine sounded like she really wanted to hire me but just couldn't since I had lied.

I finished rolling the blunt and replayed the movie. My options were gone. Well, tomorrow I'll just start over, I decided. I lit the Dutch and got comfortable and smoked like a man in misery. I felt like the unluckiest man alive.

The once interesting movie had gone to a color block screen and I was still half drunk. The powerful Mary Jane, combined with the cheap beer, made me contemplate suicide. I smoked the blunt until I became horny from the memories of all the pussy I could get. Especially Toni.

I called up every freak I knew that would fuck me on demand for free. I finally got through to a scallywag named Cherita. She had been the East Rock freak going on two years now, engaging in two-mans, three-mans, getting fucked on tape, and a bunch of other shit. But the con was her face. She was nicknamed the junkyard dog.

She agreed, but only if I hurried up because she had to leave for work soon. I jumped up and grabbed a bag of weed. I wanted to be nearly blind before fucking the dog-faced gremlin. I sped on I-695, hoping to catch her before she left and sped past a state trooper, who was thankfully already harassing someone else. I bobbed and weaved through traffic until I was on 702. It had only taken me seventeen minutes. Damn, I loved the performance my vehicle would put out.

I pulled up and banged on her back door because I didn't want to be seen going in the front by familiar faces in her neighborhood. She opened the door up buck naked.

"I just got out the shower. Well, come on. Hurry up," she told me. I stepped around her two unclaimed children and followed her upstairs to her filthy room. I quickly unzipped my jeans and strapped on a rubber. No kissing, touching, or even eye contact. I just bent her over and shoved my half-hard dick into her dry vagina. After working it for a minute or two, she became soaking wet, yelping like a virgin. It was only a front to make me come faster so she wouldn't be late for work. The bitch could take more meat than a Japanese steak house.

Her animated orgasm worked and I busted in a matter of minutes. She looked at the clock.

"Shit, I'm a be late fuckin' with you, Cream." I then heard a loud-ass bang at the door.

"Who dat?" I asked, suspicious.

"My baby-sitter. Would you let her in, please?" I rinsed my dick off and hopped down the steps to answer the door to another scally, Keisha, who stepped in the door with a small tote bag. Keisha was three hundred pounds with a dead eye. I was about to run out at the sight of the two-legged monster, but I started to feel bad about making Cherita late. She would have been well on her way if she hadn't waiting for me.

"Hey, Cherita, take your time. I'll take you to work," I yelled upstairs.

"Thank you, Jesus," I heard her sigh, and that made me feel good. I hated doing favors unless they gave me some sense of spiritual fulfillment.

Minutes later she came down the steps in her scanty waitress outfit.

"Where you work at?" I asked her, eyeing her costume.

"The Doggy House. That little restaurant in Dundalk," she answered me. I wanted to roll up, but I was still high and the quick orgasm had enhanced it. I hoped that no one was chilling on the block; I would never hear the end of being seen with Cherita in my car.

Driving toward Dundalk, I jokingly asked Cherita if the place was hiring.

"Yep, and on the spot, too," she told me.

"What for?"

"Dishwashers and waiters." I pondered trying my hand at this, at least to see how much they paid. I dismissed my pride and decided to at least go in and ask.

We pulled into the parking lot and she was surprised to see me tuck my shirt in and shout on a dab of some Blue Jeans cologne.

"Oh, you for real?" she asked, shocked.

"Yeah, bitch. What you think?" I answered, laughing.

I escorted her into the low-key restaurant and a huge black woman smiled at me as Cherita disappeared in the back.

"May I help you?" she asked.

"Yes, ma'am. I'm interested in the dishwasher job." I gave her a my best smile.

"Great! Another guy just quit just this morning. Here, fill out the application and you can start tomorrow." She had decided to hire me right away.

"I got the job?" I asked her joyfully.

"Yeah, honey, we need the help bad. But we can only pay six dollars an hour." My balloon at instantly getting hired deflated. That was sure to be a skimpy paycheck every week.

"How many hours a week?" I asked her.

"Twenty-five to thirty hours, son." Great. That was like one hundred eighty dollars before taxes. I finished filling out the application and gave her my best smile again, to hide my disappointment.

"I just needed to have it on file. I'm the hiring manager, so I'll see you tomorrow at three o'clock to begin your training. Next week, you'll get a schedule." She bit her fat tongue at me and winked. This fat bitch had a crush one me!

"See ya tomorrow," I promised and I left. The thought of working side by side with the hood slut puppy bothered me and I decided I would have to keep it a secret for as long as possible.

As I drove, I thought about when Cherita sighed, "Thank you, Jesus," after I had offered to take her to work. It was Jesus who had made me change my mind about leaving her and about giving her a ride. It was Jesus who made me ask about the job. His powerful spirit had a strange way of working on me. Who would have ever thought that ugly-ass Cherita had gotten me a job? I was thankful, convinced it was a blessing in disguise.

The Lord had humbled me into a dishwasher from a flashy drug dealer.

"Thank you for the job, Jesus," I said aloud. "I prayed for this. Three turned me down but you saw my pain and answered my call. It may not pay much, but it's an honest living for a change, and I thank you and I am grateful. In Jesus' name, I pray. Amen." I finished my thanks. All my worries of losing my car and going into huge debt seemed to float off my shoulders. I was still alive and healthy, and that's all that really mattered.

I decided to surprise my mother and go to church. It was 6:30 and I knew she went to the 7:00 service on Wednesday nights at her favorite church, Good Harvest Baptist.

The devil in me said, *Go home, smoke up, drink, and feel sorry for yourself for the loser job.* The angel in me was saying, *Continue to thank the Lord through prayer and good things will come to you.* I decided to listen to the angel for once and continued driving toward the church.

At 6:55 I walked into the small church, my shirt tucked in, and I spotted my mother. When she saw me she was singing, and she nearly fainted.

"My son, thank you God, thank you." Her joyous thanks at my arrival at church made tears stream down my face. I knew right then that I had made the right decision.

Chapter 26

For the next three weeks, I followed the same routine: wake up, smoke a blunt, go to work, come home, smoke a blunt, read a chapter from the Bible, and go to sleep. On Wednesdays and Sundays, I occasionally went to church before and after work. My brother respected me for working for such a low salary and he bought me a TV and a DVD Player.

It was the twelfth of April and I knew my car payment was eleven days late, but I chose to pay my lawyer his first installment instead of my car note. My brother arrived at my house, tailored in A/X, and I, on the other hand, was wearing a crisp white T-shirt, jean shorts, and a fitted cap. You would have thought he was the one going to see the lawyer.

It had been five weeks since my arrest and the state had already issued my court date for July 17. The short Jewish lawyer named Thom Rothstein sat behind his large marble desk. He was waiting for us.

He began explaining the warrant, how it had been signed because of the testimony of an informant. He said it wasn't much of a defense, since I was in my home when the raid took place.

"I talked to the prosecutor and she's offering five years, no parole." I felt my heart drop into my feet. Five years and no parole? I had never done more than a day and I had to fight in that short span. I became literally scared. I didn't know a lot of niggas uptown and doing five years in a prison would break me. I took a deep breath and closed my eyes to say a silent prayer. My brother removed a large stack of money; he had taken a donation from the big boys and had scraped up thirteen hundred dollars. I removed my wallet and took the five hundred dollars I had saved, and that left me with twelve dollars in my pocket to last me four more days until payday.

The little man counted the eighteen hundred dollars and smiled. He was assured that he would have the remaining twenty-two hundred dollars by July.

"I'll do my best, Donny. You've never been arrested before and you've been to college. That ought to show for something."

I got up and shook his hand, my entire hope thrown out the window and replaced with more agony.

My brother hugged me when we got on the elevator; he knew his little brother was in big trouble. I jumped in the passenger side of the Expo and rode in silence until I saw my car parked in front of the house. I was in outer space and my brother saw it.

"Keep your head up, Shorty, and call me if you need anything. Anything at all," he told me and I jumped out and went inside. I was thankful for my twenty-inch TV so I could at least watch the basketball game coming on, which might serve to cheer me up a little.

I read two chapters of the Bible, watched the exciting game, and smoked a half piece of blunt. I was developing my inner strength through the word of God. I found it easier to deal with adversity and different situations since I had started praying. I now expected the worst and took the good news with a grain of salt. I made the mistake of having my mail transferred to my current address, and bills came like weekly circulars. Everything was doubled and tripled because of late fees, and I realized I would never get out of debt without some kind of legal help.

After two more weeks of routine, Spartan living, I panicked and started parking my car three blocks from my house in an attempt to hide from the repo team. I knew I was two months late on my car note and I considered taking my brother up on his street job, but my conscience spoke against it. I even played with the thought of another armed robbery, but the thought of Pistol added to the chance of quickly getting caught nixed that idea and threw me back into reality.

I prayed about the situation vigorously, asking God to give me the truth and understanding. Maybe God wanted to continue to humble me by removing my car. Maybe he wanted me to relinquish the car myself and take the bus to and from work.

I'd just wait until tomorrow and ask the preacher after service what he though God was telling me. I was hoping God wanted me to keep the car, for it was truly my pride and joy. The vehicle made me look successful to outsiders, even if I wasn't.

I focused on the basketball game, the sounds soothing. I thought about all the times driving to watch Chuck play personally, with Steve and Danja. I flicked off the light and fell asleep, dreaming of making a three-point shot as the buzzer sounded.

* * *

The next day I approached the reverend after service and told him about my financial woes.

"Reverend, I come to church, don't sell drugs no more, and work. Why won't God work out a plan to keep my car?" Reverend Giles looked at me before responding.

"All the possessions you accumulated through sin, God has a way of taking them away from you when you turn your life over. The Lord wants you to start over, my son," he said, and I shook his hand. I had made up my mind.

"Thank you, Reverend. You really helped me a lot." I started to walk away but had one more question for him. "Would God make a way for me to get to work and church consistently?"

"Giving you strength in your limbs is him making a way." His response was so powerful and yet so true.

The following Monday I called a lawyer to inquire about filing for bankruptcy, for I thought it to be a complicated legal process. He basically said for me to bring him all my bills and five hundred dollars and he would handle everything. I told him about the situation with the car note and insurance costing more than I made in a month.

"Tomorrow, call up the finance people and tell them to repossess it. Don't mention you're filing for bankruptcy," he instructed me. I agreed and hung up after taking a small note of what he had said. Then I called my wealthy sister, who promised to help in any way possible.

"Hey, sis, it's Donny. How're the boys?" I asked her.

"Craig's at basketball practice and Damon is upstairs doing his homework."

"Tell him I said 'Happy Birthday' and that I'll get him a gift soon." The reality that I was too broke to even buy my nephew a birthday present shamed me.

Best to just come out with it: "Kelly, can you give me five hundred dollars so I can file for bankruptcy?"

"Yeah. I can give it to you at Damon's birthday party next weekend," she agreed. Wow, that was easy, I thought.

"Thanks so much, Kel. Love you."

"Love you, too. Bye now," she said and we hung up.

I was reluctant to give up the car on such short notice, so I decided to keep it until Monday. The next day I drove down to D.C. to tour the Smithsonian for the first time. Then I had to leave for work.

The job was so boring it was fun. All we did was put dishes in the washer and talk while the machine worked. On this particular day, Cherita and I happened to take our lunch breaks at the same time.

Cherita was so freaky she suggested a nasty idea at the spur of the moment.

"Hey, let's go to the car so I can suck that li'l-ass red dick of yours, nigga."

"Yeah, whatever bitch. Come on." She loved being called a bitch—anything other than ugly. She giggled and hopped in the backseat, taking caution not be seen. We only had thirty minutes, but the chance of being caught was slim due to my illegally tinted windows.

The best thing about Cherita was her head, a strong 8 ? on any suck-o-meter in town. She wasted no time, and basically tore my boxers pulling out my dick. My dick was big and the bitch thanked me for letting her deep throat it. I kicked back in my dirty work uniform. I sat in the front seat with the seat reclined all the way back while she bobbed from the back. I was getting paid to get a blowjob. I couldn't help but laugh.

133

Ten minutes passed and I felt myself about to blow a hot one and I moaned uncontrollably. A girl spits, a woman swallows, but dog-face woman swallows and cleans up the extras, and Rita was a dogface. Come shot on her tonsils and the bitch got excited and started moaning louder than me. She continued sucking until there were absolutely no traces of come left. I wanted to take the day off, smoke a blunt, and doze off in my car, but we had only twelve minutes left on break, so I fixed myself and got out. I thought about making her wait for me to get off, for the dishwasher always had to stay to clean-up—a task so nerve wracking I understood their high turnover of employees.

The place was always a mess. Naw, I decided. It would take too long and them niggas would be suspicious if she was waiting around for me. Before returning back to work, I kissed my real girlfriend—my car. That was probably the last time I would get head in my whip.

* * *

Sunday after church I informed the reverend that this was the last day of me owning the car. He smiled and patted my back.

"It's only metal and rubber. You'll own another one; just keep God first." With that I left out and went home. I pulled up in front of my house and just sat there in my car. I would take every precious moment I had left, reflecting on all the memories in the car.

The car had made me a bona fide player. I ran in the house, grabbed a blunt that was already rolled and waiting for me, and ran back to the car. I blasted Marvin Gaye and smoked my last blunt of chiva with my baby girl. I was truly going to miss my beautiful car. More tears rolled down my face. This was the final chapter in my ownership of her. I could now actually say that my involvement with the sale of marijuana had cost me every single thing that was important to me. My barrel of assets had been milked dry.

I cried while listening to the music and bobbing my head, watching the smoke float around my head. All I did these days was smoke weed, cry, and sleep. Stress told me to get high, and then I got depressed, and the combination of the two was kicking my ass. I decided to spend my last night with the car, sleeping on its butter-soft interior. I listened to the music, reclined back ,and thought about any and everything that came to mind. An hour later, I was sound asleep.

* * *

The next morning, I gathered all my personal belongings out of the car, from my CD book to my basketball in the trunk. I became emotional, realizing that this was really the end. I grabbed seventy cents for a phone call and left out.

I called the people in charge of repos and wrote down their address. I then called Braino, who agreed to follow me to drop the car off. We arrived at the place faster than I would have preferred.

My car sounded like she was crying, not even riding like her usual smooth self. I pulled up to the Perwinkle auction and removed my license plates with a screwdriver. I went inside and handed over the keys and signed four different release forms. The process didn't even take five minutes.

I would now have to rely on public transportation and free rides. I was eliminating an expensive gas bill and I should have been happy, but it only made me feel worse. I had enjoyed hustling around for gas money. My baby was well worth it. Braino's luxurious Benz didn't help matters either, although the car was designed to provide the utmost comfort to the rider. Braino felt sorry for me and tried to cheer me up with monetary donations.

"Hey, how much you owe your lawyer?" he asked helpfully.

"I just gave him another five hundred dollars, so now it's only eighteen hundred dollars," I answered pathetically. Fuck that lawyer. Fuck him, fuck everyone. I had lost my sunshine and my whole world had turned dark.

"Here. This should help you out." He handed me five big-faced clams (hundreds). "I didn't forget that good deal you gave me," he said, referring to the ounce of wood for the .380.

"Oh yeah. Don't mention it," I told him. I was thankful for his donation. I asked him to drop me off at my lawyer's office. "Okay, man, 143, man, thanks for the scratch. You guys are really coming through for me," I hugged him and got out on St. Paul. *I might as well get used to the bus,* I thought with sorrow. I took the elevator up to the beautiful law office, and the cute secretary, surprised to see me, informed my attorney that I had shown up for an unscheduled visit.

"Come on in, Donny. That's funny, I was just calling your mom's house yesterday, looking for you."

I pulled out the money, still warm from Brain's pocket, and tossed it on the desk. "We're down to thirteen, my man," I said.

"Thank you," he responded. Lawyers have a way of showing their intentions. A concerned look will go to a Kool-Aid smile the minute money was on the table. Sheer greed.

"Listen, Don. I talked to the prosecutor yesterday and she wants to talk to you tomorrow at twelve. Can you make it?"

I was picturing getting interrogated or questioned about the murders. "Yeah," I said.

"Then meet me here at ten 'til. We'll walk across the street to her office together."

"What's up? Why does she wanna talk to me?" I asked.

"I don't know. We'll see tomorrow," he said.

"All right, then. See you tomorrow." I got up, hoping that the sacrifices I was making to pay this fancy-ass lawyer would pay up in court.

I left out and headed toward the 27 bus stop, which conveniently let off two blocks from my doorstep.

* * *

I didn't have to be to work until 3:00 P.M., so I figured I'd talk with the prosecutor for an hour and then I would take the hour-and-a-half bus ride to Dundalk. I met my lawyer at 11:45. I didn't sleep at all last night, thinking about what the prosecutor could want to talk to me about.

We walked into the courthouse and disappeared down a long hallway after being frisked for weapons. The office we entered was small but tastefully decorated and comfortable.

"Just sit here, Don, she'll be a minute," my lawyer told me and I compiled. I stared at the three large plaques on her walls. One was her undergrad degree from Georgetown; her law degree was from there was well; and she had a doctorate from Johns Hopkins. So basically she was walking law genius. I was fascinated and I was fantasizing about the day I would become successful when she walked in.

She was a short, stumpy woman with short curly hair and glasses. She came in toting a huge briefcase.

"Okay, hey. Thom and Mr. Wise, I'm on a twenty-minute recess, so I have to make this quick." She thrust her hand at me and I gave her a firm shake, hoping to impress her with my manners and charm.

"Mr. Wise, do you understand that conviction of the charges pending against you could lead to some very long time?" she bluntly asked me. I nodded and she continued. "Well, listen. I checked your background and it's flawless. You've even been to college, I see, so, Mr. Wise, I don't want to send you to prison. I actually feel sorry for you." She laughed at this and went on. "So listen up. I'm gonna propose a deal. If you accept, you'll walk away whistling with a PBJ. If not, well, you'll go to prison. The deal is this: You have access to two guys we really want. Damion "Wink" Long and Leonard Mays. How do we know? Because we had the cell phone company send copies of your previous six bills. You do quite a bit of calling," she chuckled at this. "Anyway, we have had these guys in our hands, but they keep slipping through, and we want you to set up a controlled buy with either one of them for three ounces of cocaine or twenty pounds of marijuana. You'll never have to testify in court and you'll be given an informant number. Nobody will have a clue, just like you don't know who told on you."

My lawyer piped in, "Don, it's a sweet deal. She's giving you the chance to resume your life. A PBJ isn't a conviction, you can still join the service or anything else you want." I took in this deal and really thought it about it wholeheartedly. I didn't really know Wink, but Lenny was my direct connect. I knew damn well I could get away with setting up either one.

"Mrs. Lumpkin, I really appreciate your offer, but I . . . have no intention or interest in becoming an informant for the state. I really do want to resume my life, but everything happens for a reason, so it must be meant for me to go to prison." Both she and my lawyer were looking at me as if I had just started speaking Greek. I continued, "If I tell on someone, I'll be in prison forever—mentally, socially, and my soul will be scarred with betrayal. I'm sorry. I understand I don't have much of a defense, but Mr. Rothstein, I'm paying you the money that I eat with. I could have informed and got a public defender. Why would I pay you four thousand dollars then tell when they've asked me to tell since day one for free. I go too many

136

nights hungry in order to pay your fee." I couldn't believe it. I was livid that my lawyer was begging the state of mercy.

"Well, look, Mr. Wise, I'll tell you what: I'll drop the handgun charge, which carries five/no parole, if you plead guilty to PWID and accept a twenty-four month sentence at DOC to begin July 17. That's the best I can do for you. I understand that your life is at stake and you don't wann turn on your friends, but just remember that we'll get them eventually, whether you help us or not. So you might as well help." She tried to get me one more time.

"Well, Mrs. Lumpkin, good luck. If you'll excuse me, I have to catch a long bus ride to work." I started looking at my watch.

"Okay. Listen, Donny, take my card. The offer will stay on the table until June thirteith. If I don't hear from you by then, expect to be detained on the seventieth of July." I took her card from her but got up and shook hands with my lawyer.

"I'll be ready for prison on the seventieth." I told them both and walked out.

Chapter 27

Without the convenience of my vehicle, weeks passed like days. It seemed as if the long bus rides and the inability to travel reliably had taken a huge toll on me. All I did was work and sleep; even buying weed became difficult at times. No longer able to come and go as I pleased, I was forced to interact with people in my neighborhood. I smoked black' n'milds like cigarettes these days, and the more I was seen walking to the store, basketball courts, or bus stops, the more people inquired about me.

It was May 23, and I had a bankruptcy hearing on Pratt Street at 3:00. I had to call in to work for the day off, but it was only the second time since my hire.

The treasurer was surprised when he read my date of birth.

"You're only twenty-one and you're filing for bankruptcy?" he asked, incredulous, his voice scratchy.

"Yes sir. You don't know the half of it." I tried to be candid with him. My total debt was thirty thousand; I owed fourteen thousand on the car alone. My lawyer, Mr. Fillmore, informed me of my rights and explained the procedure to me.

The room was filled with diversity: Seventy-year old widows and young interracial couples. It made me feel good to know that everyone of all different shades and ages had financial difficulties at one point or another. A representative from a credit card company came to dispute my claim.

"Don't worry about her. As long as you don't have over six thousand in cash and property assets, she can't touch you. Chapter 7 is the easiest of the three to get approved," Mr. Fillmore assured me.

After swearing to tell the truth about being broke, the Treasurer spoke for a minute or two and then stamped a paper, shook my hand, and told me "Good luck." This whole process was recorded on a giant machine and I was told I would receive a clearance form in ninety days.

I walked out, shook my lawyer's hand, and then headed to the closet bar to get smashed. And I did. I was celebrating for having my slate wiped clean but also to soften the finality of my decision. It would be seven years before my credit report was cleared, I drank shots of tequila until the room looked blurry and then I staggered out to the street. I hopped the Lite Rail and went home, singing "The Dance Is Over" the whole way. I somehow made it home; I was having trouble holding my bladder for the four blocks it was to my house from the Lite Rail station.

I was intoxicated to the highest degree and I prayed for sobriety. After showering, throwing up, then showering again, my head spun so fast I was nauseated. I lay on my tiny bed, butterball naked, and laughed until I was tired. Then I masturbated until I was soaking wet with sweat and come and rolled over on my stomach to pass out so I wouldn't vomit in my sleep and drown my damn self.

"Man, get yo naked ass up!" I opened one eye and saw my brother. "Come on yo!" He was anxious.

"Why? What's up?" I asked groggily.

"Man, you left your front door open, piss all in the vestibule. What the hell is wrong with you?" he scolded me.

"Man, I drank tequila last night for the first time in my life. Need I say more?" I said and rolled over.

"Man, get up. We're having a party for my son and Black's son at 5:30. Everyone is downstairs waiting for you." The thought of not being left out of a major thing gave me strength in my bones. A birthday party for a black kid was really a front for his parents to get smashed. Any occasion was an excuse to turn up the stereo, break out the grill, and fill the coolers with beer and the back room with weed.

I dressed in the new clothes I had bought from a hard up booster at Mondawmin Mall. I was already twizzy, but I always had room for free weed and food these days. I stumbled twice and nearly broke my neck trying to walk down the narrow stairs. My dogs greeted me with ridicule.

"Pissy wu wu!"

"You non drinking motherfucker!"

"Get yo yellow ass up, puck!'

"Nigga, we gonna make yo ass dance naked in the street," Matt yelled, pulling out a bottle of Dom and a ounce of hydro. Black was already smoking a blunt and he practically shoved it in my mount. I hit it hard while he held it to my lips. The strong weed hit me like a Teflon right hook and I choked my lungs up.

The boys started laughing loudly. "Nigga, that's dro and skunk mixed together. Called 'drunk', cause after three hits you feel drunk," Black sang out. I couldn't tell, I thought it was just commercial until I coughed so hard tears streamed down my face and I started gagging.

At this, we all left together. Braino brandished his new truck, an '01 Tahoe; Black and my brother rode in Rock's long ass LTD; and Matt was driving his hoopdee, his Cutlass Sierra. I hopped in the car with Matt, although I wanted to check out Braino's new toy. We drove along, smoking on commercial and talking about life.

139

Matt was expecting his third child and was contemplating marrying his girl-friend, Renee.

"Man, three kids by the same woman, Cream, I might as well go ahead and put that rock on her finger."

"Yeah, well, with them beautiful mixed babies, I don't see why not," I said, grimacing from swallowing because my throat was so sore from all the hacking earlier. The rest of the ride we just listened to Jill Scott sing relaxing music and I must have dozed off.

"Nigga, get yo drunk ass up!" Matt was pushing my shoulder, and I opened my eyes and sat up and saw that we were at Black's house. We always used Black's house for parties. It had an enclosed backyard and a kerosene grill. The party was for a one and two year old, but the backyard was for the grown ups.

The dining room was decorated with party hats and a huge birthday cake, and little party bags lay next to each plate and napkin setting. There were balloons all over the living room, and the table and sofa had been removed to create more space for the guests.

Ten little midgets ran throughout the huge house, playing with any and everything they could find. I was happy to see my son running around with the kids, for it had been three months since I had seen him last. My baby mother, still upset over the arrest, had avoided my phone calls and had eventually changed her number. It was only by the grace of God that Dan had somehow made it to the party.

An entire corner of the living room was designated for the gifts for the two birthday kids. Lil' Deionya and Lil' Rock were born a year apart on the same day. It was fitting that best friends' sons shared birthdays.

I picked up Dan, holding in my emotions; I wanted to crush him to my chest, cry, and never let go. Dan had grown up a little and was starting to look like a toddler.

"I miss you, Daddy," he said into my neck, still clinging tightly to me. He usually called me Donny, unless he was in trouble or sad. I knew the separation was hurting him and this upset me greatly. I squeezed him into my chest, whispering how sorry I was for leaving him. I finally let him down and he took off behind his little cousins.

I saw Matt's two kids hiding, and I snatched them each up and kissed both of them because Matt had made me their unofficial godfather. This reunion with the kids made me regret my numbered days on the outside. I knew that in five weeks I would be in prison. I searched for Braino's daughter, who was a spitting image of her mother, and I knew exactly where to find her: sitting on Braino's lap, clinging to his waist. She was the definition of Daddy's Little Girl.

I felt a strong blow to my back and whipped around to see my oldest nephew Craig, who was eleven and almost as tall as me. He was a basketball nut and he sported an Iverson jersey.

"Did you see the game where Ive—" but I cut him off. The boy was a walking sports almanac and we often talked on the phone for hours about sports.

"Where's Damon?" I asked him.

"Over there somewhere," he said, playing with his long braids. I went to the direction in which he pointed and found my little man Damon holding on to Lil' Rock's hand. Damon was six year old with a twelve year old's mentality. He was so articulate, it made the average person laugh and feel inadequate. He often saw right through old adult fakes like Santa Claus, the Tooth Fairy, and the Easter Bunny. He once came to me and said, "Uncle Donny, if Santa slides down our chimney, he will get locked up!" When I asked him why, he told me, "We have an alarm system, no chimney, and my mother always tells Craig to lock the doors when he gets sleepy." I couldn't help but laugh at this; this kid was sharp.

The good thing was it reflected onto his schoolwork and he was a straight A student and spoiled rotten because of it. I bent down to hug Lil Rock and kissed his fat little cheeks. He had on a baby Coogi sweater that hung to his baby Timberlands. He was an identical twin of his father; they looked like a mirror image of each other. I searched around for Deionya and found him upstairs playing with Daniel. Deionya loved to dance around and his chubby little body made his movements hilarious. He was adorable with pretty hair and brown eyes and he, too, was a miniature version of his father.

After making the rounds to see my "kids," I went to the backyard to enjoy the adult festivities. Everyone was sitting around looking like zombies from the strong weed. We partied hard and Rock kept everyone amused, as per his usual self. He was a natural comedian. He was imitating the way his friend Tito, with the lisp, talked. Everyone was almost hysterical with laughter.

For the first time in five months, I felt happy. Actually happy. My friends were having a good time and everyone was showing each other love; it felt good to be a part of it. I started smoking the Dutches and drinking the expensive champagne until it was time to do the cake and sing "Happy Birthday" to the kids.

On the drive home I broke down to Matt, telling him how much I loved my friends and their families. He just told me to shut up because I was drunk and talking stupid. His unsentimental comment to my moment of trying to pour my heart out made my laugh like hell. I couldn't stop giggling, because leave it to Matt to bring us all back to reality.

I hugged him when we pulled up to my house. I had clipped a handful of weed and had enough to roll two blunts. I was going to need to smoke, because the reality of leaving my family and friends for prison was riding on my head.

I prayed that God would keep me strong during this time of need I had truly enjoyed the last gathering I would have with my best friends and family in awhile. I missed Steve terribly; his parents had changed their number and moved into a small townhouse in order to pay his legal fees. I prayed for the Lord to make a way for him.

I rolled up the weed, but for some reason, something told me not to smoke anymore. I contemplated this thoroughly and then I eventually flushed the weed down the toilet. I would try to stay sober until my departure. Maybe it was the Lord telling me that enough was enough. I fell asleep, praying for the strength to kick my mind-altering habit.

Chapter 28

The ambiance of the party stayed with me for the next seven weeks. I ate better, laughed more, and found myself behaving more like a man of God. It was July 17 and I found myself in high spirits, despite what was to happen today.

Miraculously, I had lost the urge to drink and get high since the birthday party. I woke at 7:30 A.M. showered thoroughly, and dressed respectably, though I knew that by nightfall, I would be in prison orange.

I saved my mother the trouble of packing my small wardrobe and pictures sent to me from the memorial party. I left a small note to my mother, brother, and son saying how much I loved them and how much better my love would show upon my release. I wrote a small thank you note to "Show Daddy," for he had let me slide on July's rent.

I opened the Bible to 2 Corinthians 1:1-11 and said a lengthy prayer, expressing my thanks. I took one last look at the room I had grown to like and left out. I was ready to face the consequences for my actions. I walked to the nearest main street and flagged a cab down.

When the cab driver pulled over, he asked my destination in a nasty tone.

"Take me to jail, please," I answered him, as friendly as he was nasty. We arrived at the courthouse and I was still early, so I went and had my last breakfast at my favorite spot. To lighten my sprits, I bought five dollars worth of lotto tickets. Nobody in the café understood why I laughed while asking how long I had to cash the winning ticket. Six months.

I walked to the front of the courthouse, inhaling my last few breaths of fresh air. The sun was shining so bright on this day. The birds were singing and flowers were blossoming. I promised to never take the small things in life for granted again. I checked my watch, and my hour had finally come to hear my fate.

I walked with confidence to Courtroom 228, part 16. My mother, all decked out in a blue pin-striped suit, sat in the third row from the back. I was saddened by what I was about to put her through, seeing her youngest child dragged away in handcuffs. I sat beside her and hugged her with everything I had before handing her the keys to my door and my wallet.

"You can have the two hundred inside, Ma," I told her.

"Boy, quit playin' around. You ain't going nowhere," she told me.

"Yeah, Mother, I am." I was okay with this and God's strength made me accept what was to come. He had blessed me with a stable mind able to deal with my worst fear and had almost made me look forward to it.

My lawyer came in, followed by the prosecutor, Mrs. Lumpkin, and we made eye contact before she told the bailiff that a sheriff would be needed. "We have two detainees. Marcus Wilson and Don-ny Wise." She amplified the syllables of my name loud enough for me to hear her. She took her place and laid down the large ratty briefcase she toted around.

The judge came out of his chambers and the whole room rose for his presence. My lawyer and the prosecutor immediately approached the bench after his bailiff had motioned everyone to be seated. They conversed for a few minutes before my lawyer walked back to me and took his place at the defense table.

The prosecutor called out, "The State versus Donny Wise, case number 1099171," and I nudged my lawyer.

"Don't worry, the judge is going to recommend boot camp," he said in my ear and the prosecutor began to explain the plea agreement. I had assurance that God would not allow me to sit in a prison for long, no matter what the judge recommended.

The Honorable, a white man in his mid sixties, read the plea silently before asking if I wanted to say anything before my sentencing.

"Yes, Your Honor. First of all, I am sorry, Mother, for what I am putting you through. Please forgive me. Second, I would like to apologize to the courts because I should have know better. And last, I would like to thank God for putting me through this transition early on in life. He sees my faults and promises to correct them. He has instilled his inner strength in me. Thank You, Your Honor, that is all," I finished up.

"Okay, young man," he answered. "We, the court, sentence you to twenty-four months at the Department of Corrections. As an accommodation to your youth and your lack of a record, I will recommend you for boot camp. Good luck, Mr. Wise." And he tapped his gavel twice. I heard hysterical screams and saw my mother, who was nearly fainting, watching the sheriff snap the cuffs on my wrists. *Please, God, give me strength, please, God give me strength,* I prayed, watching my mother cry with pain.

"No! Two years! No! That's my baby! Noooo!" Two bailiffs had to restrain her from grabbing me as I was escorted out. Tears circled my eyes as I watched the dramatic outburst unfold. My lawyer escorted me to the door and slipped a card in my pocket.

"That's my house number. Call me if you need anything at all," he told me, and now that this was all over, I felt a sense of relief. I didn't feel lonely anymore, and the thought of my new life with Christ excited me.

No longer would my life be judged by my past mistakes. I was now free to move on. I remembered what the reverend had told me after service that one day: "The Lord is taking everything you accumulated through sin and getting rid of it in order for you to start over by putting Him first." It was now making even more sense; my evil ways and habits had been accentuated because of sin. My mental addiction was attributed to sin. God was going through the steps of changing my wretched sin-filled life.

By incarcerating my old self, he was ridding my soul of my old spirit, and it was up to me to come out a new person, with a perspective on life. His powerful spirit was cleaning and changing my mind about living. I felt this was His way of getting my mind right, by taking away all my earthly possessions, even my freedom, so that I would come to Him empty and broke and beg to be filled up with his love. My priorities needed to be rearranged. I needed to put God first.

I promised to take this time to learn about God and return back to society with a new outlook. I looked forward to the transformation as the sheriff led me into the bullpen and removed the handcuffs. I vowed to leave my old spirit behind the jailhouse bars forever.